·TALES OF A·
KOREAN
GRANDMOTHER

·TALES OF A·
KOREAN
GRANDMOTHER

FRANCES CARPENTER

TUTTLE Publishing

Tokyo | Rutland, Vermont | Singapore

The Tuttle Story: "Books to Span the East and West"

Most people are surprised to learn that the world's largest publisher of books on Asia had its beginnings in the tiny American state of Vermont. The company's founder, Charles E. Tuttle, belonged to a New England family steeped in publishing. And his first love was naturally books—especially old and rare editions.

Immediately after WW II, serving in Tokyo under General Douglas MacArthur, Tuttle was tasked with reviving the Japanese publishing industry, and founded the Charles E. Tuttle Publishing Company, which thrives today as one of the world's leading independent publishers.

Though a westerner, Charles was hugely instrumental in bringing knowledge of Japan and Asia to a world hungry for information about the East. By the time of his death in 1993, Tuttle had published over 6,000 books on Asian culture, history and art—a legacy honored by the Japanese emperor with the "Order of the Sacred Treasure," the highest tribute Japan can bestow upon a non-Japanese.

With a backlist of 1,500 titles, Tuttle Publishing is more active today than at any time in its past—inspired by Charles' core mission to publish fine books to span the East and West and provide a greater understanding of each.

Published by Tuttle Publishing, an imprint of Periplus Editions (HK) Ltd.

www.tuttlepublishing.com

Copyright in Japan, 1973
by Charles E. Tuttle Publishing Company, Inc.
All rights reserved.

Library of Congress Catalog Card No.
72077515
ISBN: 978-0-8048-1043-2

First edition published 1947
by Doubleday & Company, Inc., Garden City, N.Y.

First Tuttle edition, 1973
Printed in Singapore

12 13 14 15   22 21 20 19   1112TP

TUTTLE PUBLISHING® is a registered trademark of Tuttle Publishing, a division of Periplus Editions (HK) Ltd.

Distributed by:

Japan
Tuttle Publishing
Yaekari Building, 3rd Floor
5-4-12 Osaki, Shinagawa-ku, Tokyo 141-0032
Tel: (81) 3 5437-0171; Fax: (81) 3 5437-0755
sales@tuttle.co.jp
www.tuttle.co.jp

North America, Latin America & Europe
Tuttle Publishing
364 Innovation Drive
North Clarendon, VT 05759-9436 U.S.A.
Tel: 1 (802) 773-8930; Fax: 1 (802) 773-6993
info@tuttlepublishing.com
www.tuttlepublishing.com

Asia Pacific
Berkeley Books Pte. Ltd.
61 Tai Seng Avenue, #02-12, Singapore 534167
Tel: (65) 6280-1330; Fax: (65) 6280-6290
inquiries@periplus.com.sg
www.periplus.com

To my favorite children
DAVID and JOANNA

TABLE

OF

CONTENTS

TABLE OF CONTENTS

LIST

OF

ILLUSTRATIONS

LIST OF ILLUSTRATIONS

ACKNOWLEDGMENT

THE popular folk tales which have been adapted in this book have been collected from many sources. Among these special mention should be made of the early English-language periodicals, *The Korean Repository* and *The Korean Review,* and of the writings of the missionaries, teachers, and travelers in Korea during the last decades of the nineteenth century, as follows: *Corea, the Hermit Nation* by William Elliot Griffis; *Korean Tales* by Horace Newton Allen; *Life in Corea* by W. R. Carles; *Korea and Her Neighbors* by Isabella Bird Bishop; the works of James S. Gale; the articles and books of Homer B. Hulbert; *Korean Games* by Stewart Culin.

Much valuable material was found in the early writings of the author's father, Frank G. Carpenter, who visited Korea first in 1888, and with whom she herself traveled there in the days before that unhapy country was annexed by Japan.

The author also wishes to express gratitude to Pyo Wook Han, Korean scholar and critic, for assistance in checking the accuracy of her pictures of family life in Old Korea.

THE

HOUSE

OF

KIM

THE Korean grandmother sat comfortably on the soft tiger-skin rug, enjoying the autumn breeze that drifted in through the open door of her apartment. She puffed contentedly at her long pipe while she watched two of her granddaughters playing on the seesaw out in the walled courtyard. The girls were laughing and squealing as they stood upright, one on each end of a board laid across a firm sack of earth. Their long, bright-colored skirts flew like banners in the wind. Their jet-black braids, tied with little red bows, swung back and forth as they jumped up and down so as to toss each other high into the air.

But again and again the old woman's dark eyes were turned away from their play. They sought instead the gateway on the far side of the Inner Court, beside the long, low building which housed the men of the Kim family and which protected the women's quarters from the outer entrance court. Like the little girl who stood just outside her door on the narrow veranda, the woman seemed to be listening for some special sound.

"The men should be coming home, Halmoni," the child said, retying the red ribbons that fastened the short green jacket above her long, very full rose-colored skirt.

"*Yé*, they should be returning, little Ok Cha," her grandmother replied. "The sun has dropped down behind our garden wall. The evening bell soon will be struck. The great gates of the city will swing together. If the Master of this House does not make haste, he and the others will spend the night on the highway."

It had seemed strange all day to Ok Cha, with her father and her uncles, her brothers and her boy cousins, all gone from the walled courts of the Kim household. It was the time of the autumn Feast of the Ancestors, when prayers and thanksgivings must be offered at the family grave mounds out on the hills that encircled their city of Seoul. And, of course, only menfolk were important enough to take part in such a ceremony.

That morning, at sunrise, a little procession had gone forth from the bamboo gate. Leading it was Kim Hong Chip, father of Ok Cha and oldest son of this Korean grandmother, whom everyone called "Halmoni." Ever since his father's death, Kim Hong Chip had borne the important title, Master of the House. In all family ceremonies he was the leader.

Kim Hong Chip was a fine-looking, dignified man. On this day he was clad as usual in a spotless white jacket and white baggy pantaloons tied neatly about his ankles above his thick-soled quilted shoes. Over all he had on his best long green coat that gleamed like silk in the sun. Through the meshes of his tall black hat of woven horsehair his trim topknot showed, standing straight up through the opening of his black gauze skullcap.

As befitted the master of a *yangban*, or noble family such as the Kims, he rode out of the city, perched on a sturdy little Korean horse. A servant trotted along beside him, at hand to steady his portly, well-fed body over the rough places in the narrow country road. Another servant ran ahead, shouting loudly to the less important wayfarers, "Make way! Make way! A great man comes!"

Halmoni's younger sons and grandsons, dressed just like the Master, hurried to keep their places in the procession. By their topknots it was easy to tell which ones were married, for each boy and bachelor in Korea then wore his well-oiled black hair in one long braid down his back.

Last of all came the menservants, with brooms to tidy the grave site and with loads of wine, rice cakes, and puddings to please the ancestors' spirits. Later, when the prayers all had been said, these good things pleased also their descendants, who picnicked upon them in the family pavilion near by.

"It is good to be born a boy like Yong Tu," Ok Cha said wistfully, coming to sit down at her grandmother's side. The little girl envied her brother—not because he was the oldest son of their father and thus one day would become, like him, Master of the House, but just because Yong Tu was a boy. He could do so many things that were not permitted then to girls in Korea. He could walk on the street. He could picnic on the hills in the spring, or fly kites out there when the winter winds blew. He could even go with his father or the servants to buy toys in the markets and stores of the city.

Ok Cha, now that she was a full eight years old, would not be allowed to set foot outside the Inner Court. She would not see the city streets except through the curtains of the sedan chair in which she might go visiting with her mother. When she was married, she would only exchange the Inner Court of her father's house for that of her husband.

It was not that the little Korean girl was unhappy. These were the customs all over her land. Omoni, her busy mother, and Halmoni always found ways to occupy and amuse themselves in the Inner Court. Oh, it was pleasant there, and one could play also in the Garden of Green Gems behind the women's houses. Ok Cha knew the Inner Court was far safer for girls than the city streets with their crowds of rough men.

Ok Cha, Yong Tu, and their grandmother, as well as the other people in this story, lived many, many years ago. That was before western ideas and new ways of living came to this Asiatic land of Korea. Because it had long refused to let foreign traders or travelers land on its shores, Korea was nicknamed the "Hermit Kingdom." A hermit among the nations it was, shut off to itself like a frog in a well and knowing almost nothing of the great world beyond its seacoasts.

"Our 'Little Kingdom' is like a bone between two dogs," Halmoni used to explain. "Mighty China, to the north and west, and strong Japan, to the east, would like to swallow it up." She told her grandchildren that by sending thousands of bags of rice and boatloads of rich silk each year to China, their land bought its freedom to live in peace. Thus it bought also the help of China in keeping away its greedy neighbor, Japan. It was only when Japan became so much stronger than China that it was able to conquer Korea. Halmoni would have been sad indeed if the blind fortune-teller she so often consulted had foretold the long sad years when her land was to be under Japanese rule. These were to last until Korea was set free by World War II.

Some say Korea's ancient name of Chosun means "Land of Morning Calm." Others like better "Land of Morning Brightness." In a household like that of the Kims, there were, in those times, many bright days and many calm days, like this Day of the Ancestors.

But it was never really quiet in the Inner Court of the rich Kim household. There was the constant rat-a-tat-tat of the ironing sticks in the hands of the maidservants. In this land the women, as well as the men, wore chiefly garments of white grass linen—short white jackets and long white trousers or very full white skirts. The boys and the girls had similar clothes of gayer hues—pale blues, bright greens, and rosy pinks. There was always something to be washed clean and pounded smooth on the flat oblong ironing stones.

There were always sounds, too, coming out of the kitchen. Just now twigs and leaves were being stuffed into the fireplace there, to keep the rice water boiling and to make sure plenty of hot air would flow out from the stove under the floors of the houses. The travelers would be hungry and cold. When they dropped down to rest, they must feel the warmth of the stone floors through the smooth oiled-paper coverings.

"What is it that has only one mouth and yet has three necks?" This was a riddle about the kitchen fireplace which Ok Cha liked to ask. The firebox was the mouth, of course. The three necks were the flues which brought heat from the firebox out under the floors and thus warmed the houses.

The great city bell was booming its evening warning when the Master of the House was lifted down from his pony. Yong Tu and the other boys ran at once to the Inner Court to bring their mothers and Halmoni the flaming autumn leaves they had picked out on the hills, and to tell them of the day's doings.

But the women were busy making ready the evening meal for their husbands and sons. Large bowls were heaped high with steaming rice. Smaller bowls were being filled with bean sauce, fish, and the savory pickle called *kimchee*. All these bowls were arranged on tiny low tables, to be set down on the floor near each hungry man. For drinking, there were bowls of steaming rice water. In Korea, in those days, cows were raised for drawing plows or carrying loads, not for giving milk.

Only when the menfolk had been fed, and the women and girls had themselves eaten, did the family begin to move across the Inner Court to Halmoni's apartment. The Hall of Perfect Learning, the room where the Master received his men guests, was larger. The Hall of the Ancestors was finer. But Halmoni's room was the true center of the Kim household. From her place, here in the Inner Court, she directed the lives of all of her family. Because of her age, and because they loved her so much, she was the true head of the House of Kim.

As was the custom of those times, three of her sons had brought their brides to live in the Kim family courtyards. Here all their children were being brought up. There was ample room for them all, for the houses of the Kims were among the richest and most spacious in all the capital city of Seoul. Their curving tiled roofs stood out proudly in the sea of grass roofs of the more ordinary houses.

The plaster walls of the Kim houses were smoother, and their fine paper windows let in more light, than those of its neighbors. In few other homes in Seoul were there more handsome brassbound clothing chests, more elegantly embroidered screens, nor more scholarly wall writings. Halmoni specially treasured the thick tiger skins which had covered the official sedan chair of her dead husband.

In the Master's Hall of Perfect Learning, behind little panels in the walls, there were precious books and rolls of white paper upon which poems had been set down with the skillful brush strokes of scholars.

"Always, Yong Tu, there have been poets and scholars in our family," Halmoni sometimes said to her grandson. "Next it is you who must bring such honor to our house. Like your grandfather and your great-grandfather, you must learn to make the golden words flow off your rabbit-hair brush. You must become a *paksa* like them, a true 'master of wisdom.' To be a *paksa* is to mount the dragon of good luck, blessed boy. One day you, too, shall pass the Emperor's examinations. You, too, shall win high office, fortune, and fame."

Each day the old woman helped Yong Tu with his lessons. Halmoni knew how to read and write *unmun*, the "people's language," whose words were formed with the letters of the Korean alphabet. But by helping her own sons and her grandsons, she had learned also many of the sayings of the old Chinese scholars. The stories Halmoni told the children often sounded as fine to them as the poems their father wrote in his Hall of Perfect Learning.

It was Halmoni who had chosen the poetic names of her grandchildren. Ok Cha loved her name which meant "Jade Child," for everyone knew that smooth gleaming jade is the most precious of stones. Yong Tu was proud to be called "Dragon Head," because a dragon is the most splendid of all the beasts and his name was sure to bring good luck.

Yong Tu was glad he did not have a name like that of his baby brother, whom Halmoni called "Little Pig." That name was only for his baby years, to be sure. It was chosen to fool the spirits into thinking he was not worthy of being carried away. Later it would be changed to a more honorable title, perhaps "Fierce Leopard" or "Great Mountain."

When the pipes were lighted and everyone was squatting at ease on mats on the warm floor, Kim Hong Chip began to tell Halmoni about the events of the Ancestors' Feast.

"Our grave mounds are well placed," he began. "The sun falls upon them from the south, and the hills lead to them like the waving back of a dragon. No 'spying peak' peers down upon them over the ridge. The hills opposite stand up straight and firm, like men set there to protect them. The Honorable Ancestors' spirits should be well pleased, and good luck should live with us."

Their duty to their ancestors was even more important to Koreans than the honor they paid their living parents. The Kims all believed that each person who "mounted the dragon to Heaven" took only one of his three souls with him. A second dwelt in the grave mound. A third rested in his little white wooden tablet in the ancestors' apartment in the family courts. On the appointed days of the year, the Master, with his oldest son at his side, knelt in this Tablet House. They bowed their heads to the floor, saying the family prayers. The need for sons to carry on these ceremonies for the ancestors was one reason why boys in Korea were thought to be so much more important than their sisters.

Ok Cha and Yong Tu always jumped to do their father's bidding. They stood in awe of this dignified man, whose word was law in their house. He never paid much attention to them nor showed how much he loved them, for that would be boasting.

The children ran quickly also when their grandmother called, but that was because they liked so well to be with her. Their greatest pleasure was to sit by her side and listen to the strange tales she brought forth from the treasure house of her memory.

Halmoni knew by heart stories about the ancient Chinese teacher, Confucius. She could tell of the adventures of the good Buddha, who lived long ago in India, over the mountains far beyond China. But the stories her grandchildren liked best were about the spirits and animals of their own land—the fierce tiger kings of the mountains, the good river dragons, and the *tokgabis*, mischievous little elves who hid under the curving tiled roofs.

Every mishap in the household the children blamed on these *tokgabis*, poor wandering spirits who had never found their way up to heaven. A tear in a paper windowpane, a lid falling into a boiling pot, the evening rice burned—all these were surely the work of the *tokgabis,* the children thought.

"If you should ever meet a *tokgabi,*" Halmoni told the children, "stand up so straight and proud that you look down upon him. Take out a bit of shining silver, a strip of red cloth, or a charm made from the wood of a lightning-struck tree. Then he will go away."

Along the ridges of the Kim roofs stood tiny clay figures of strange animals and ugly little men, put there to frighten the bad spirits away. A picture of the fat kitchen god was kept on the god shelf over the stove to prevent them from spoiling the family meals. Ok Cha and Yong Tu had learned always to step high over a threshold, lest they tread on the good guardian spirit of the house, who might be lying across it. They knew there were good spirits as well as bad. One could never be sure which were about. It was well to be careful.

As real to Halmoni and her grandchildren as their ancestors' spirits were all these unseen beings. When the old grandmother told of a man turned into an ox, of a cat whose fur dripped rice, or of a woodcutter who came upon the gods of the mountain playing at chess, they were sure such things could happen.

"I heard these tales from my own grandmother," Halmoni used to say. "How then can they not be true?"

"Always, Yong Tu, there have been poets and scholars in our family," said Halmoni. "They were true masters of wisdom who won high office at court."

24

LAND

OF

MORNING

BRIGHTNESS

I N HALMONI'S ROOM, while the others talked in the light of the fish-oil lamps, Yong Tu sat apart at a little low table. The boy had opened one of the shining wood chests and had brought out his writing tools—his little inkstone, his ink paste, and his soft, fine, rabbit-hair brush. Squatting in his corner, he bent over a long strip of white paper, upon which he was making painstaking brush strokes. No one noticed what he was doing until he stood before his grandmother, paper in hand.

"Out on the hills today, Halmoni, I thought of this poem for the Honorable Ancestors. I have set it down to show you," the boy said somewhat shyly.

On all occasions the members of the Kim family, big and little, liked to make up poems and songs. Poems were like spring blossoms, they said; they always gave pleasure. Today Yong Tu's was the best among those of all the children. His poems were usually the ones to be hung on the walls of Halmoni's room.

"Like the phoenix among fowls,
Like the tiger among beasts,
You shine in the throngs
At the Heav'nly Emperor's feasts."

"Well done, my young *paksa*," Halmoni cried when the boy had read his little poem aloud for the family. "Your arrows hit the mark as neatly as those of Chu Mong, the Skillful Archer, whom men used to call 'Light of the East.'"

"Isn't it time for that story now, Halmoni?" Ok Cha begged, looking up into the kind twinkling eyes of her old grandmother. Often on days like this when the ancestors were especially honored, the old woman liked to tell of the beginnings of their land, and of the very first ancestors of the Korean people. Among them, she always said, were persons named Kim, for their family, as everyone knew, was one of the oldest and most honorable in all the land.

"*Yé*, the Master of this House is departing. I will tell you the story. I shall speak first of Tan Kun, the Lord of the Sandalwood Tree. He came even earlier than did Chu Mong, the Skillful Archer. It was in the very beginning when our country first rose out of the sea. With its ten thousand mountain peaks on its back, our land mounted the waves like a great dragon.

"Marvels took place in those times, my children. Tan Kun was the son of a spirit from heaven and a beautiful bear-woman. His father, they say, was Han Woon, the very son of Hananim, the Lord of Heaven and Earth. When Han Woon came down to the earth, he brought with him thousands of his spirit friends. Among them were the Lord

28

of Winds, the Ruler of Rain, and the Driver of Clouds. He set up his court under a great sandalwood tree. But all in it remained spirits. They did not take on human forms like those of the wild people who then roamed over the land.

"One day a she-bear and a tiger met on the side of the Ever-White Mountains, whose peaks hold back the clouds of the northern sky. As they talked, each beast declared that his greatest wish was to become a human being and walk upright on two legs. Suddenly a voice came out of the clouds, saying, 'You have only to eat twenty-one cloves of garlic, and hide yourselves away from the sun for three times seven days. Then you will have your wish.'

"The tiger and the she-bear ate the garlic and crept in out of the sunshine, far inside a dark cave. Now the tiger is a restless creature, my little ones, and the time seemed very long. At the end of eleven days he could stand the waiting no longer. He rushed out into the sunlight. Thus that tiger, still having the form of a beast, went off to his hunting again, on all four feet.

"The she-bear was more patient. She curled up and slept throughout the thrice-seven days. On the twenty-first morning, she came forth from the cave, walking upright on two legs, like you and me. Her hairy skin dropped away, and she became a beautiful woman.

"When the beautiful bear-woman sat down to rest under the sandalwood tree, Han Woon, the Spirit King, saw her. He blew his breath upon her, and in good time a baby boy was born to them. Years later, the wild tribes found this baby boy, grown into a handsome youth, sitting under that same tree. And they called him 'Tan Kun, Lord of the Sandalwood Tree.' They made him their king, and they listened well to his words.

"The Nine Tribes of those times were rough people, my children. In summer they lived under trees, like the spirits; in winter they took shelter in caves dug in the ground. They had not yet learned how to bind up their hair, to weave themselves clothing, nor to shut their wives away from the eyes of strange men. They knew nothing of growing good rice, nor of making savory *kimchee*. Their foods were the berries and nuts, the wild fruit and roots they found in the forests."

Halmoni paused a little to take a drink of the sweet honey water she liked so much. Then she continued her story.

"Tan Kun taught these wild people to cut down the trees and to open the earth to grow grain. He showed them how to cook their rice and how to heat their houses. Under his guidance they wove cloth out of grass fibers. They learned to comb their hair neatly, into braids for the boys and girls, into topknots for the married men, and into smooth coils for their wives.

"Good ways of living thus came to this Dragon-Backed Land. Tan Kun ruled it wisely for more than one thousand years, so my father told me. Our people had already begun to grow great when our second wise ruler came. This was the Emperor Ki Ja from across the Duck Green River, from China beyond the Ever-White Mountains."

"What became of Tan Kun, Halmoni?" Yong Tu asked.

"Tan Kun was no longer needed then, blessed boy," his grandmother replied. "He became a spirit again, and he flew back up to Heaven. But men say that an altar he built to honor his grandfather, Hananim, still stands on the faraway hills to the north."

Yong Tu knew all about Ki Ja, who is often called the "Father of Korea." It was written in the boy's own history book that, more than three thousand years ago, Ki Ja was an important official in China. He was unhappy under the wicked rule of the Chinese emperor who then sat on the Dragon Throne there. So he set forth to found a kingdom where people might live more safely and in peace.

"Five thousand good Chinese accompanied Ki Ja," Halmoni told her listeners. "Among them were doctors to heal the sick, and scholars to teach the ignorant people. There were mechanics and carpenters to show how cities could be built, and fortunetellers and magicians who knew how to keep away evil spirits. Books, paintings, and musical instruments were brought with them, also the precious worms that spin silk. Ki Ja gave his new subjects the Five Laws that taught them their duties to themselves and their fellows.

"Those were golden days," Halmoni declared, shaking her head so that the silver-and-coral pin in the coil of black hair on her neck gleamed in the lamplight. "Travelers were safe from robbers on the roads. Gates could safely be kept open after nightfall. Everyone was polite and kind to his neighbor. *Hé*, it must have been good to live in those times.

"Ki Ja's tomb could still be pointed out, not far from the Peony Mountain near Pyeng Yang, the capital city that was built by Tan Kun. The pillar of rock to which people declared his first boat was moored and Ki Ja's well still stood, but they, too, were outside the city gates. Pyeng Yang was built in the shape of a boat, so it was said. Now everyone knows a boat will sink if a hole is bored in its bottom. That is why it was forbidden in those early times to dig wells inside this boat city. That is why the people there had to carry all their water such a long way."

"But what about Chu Mong, the Skillful Archer, Halmoni?" Ok Cha asked. The little girl liked his story best. And as her grandmother told it, Chu Mong's family name also had been Kim.

"*Yé*, Chu Mong, like Ki Ja, crossed the Duck Green River beneath the Ever-White Mountains. He, too, brought good ways to our land. From him came its ancient name, so my grandfather always declared. It all happened like this.

"In very early times, when Korea still was divided into many small kingdoms, there was a certain king to the north who wept because he had no son. One day during a hunt he knelt by a stream in the deep woods and prayed the Jade Emperor of Heaven to send him a son. When he rose to his feet and turned toward his horse, he was startled to see great tears rolling out of the animal's eyes. The horse was pawing and pawing at a huge gray rock at the side of the path. Suddenly the rock moved, and the horse rolled it aside.

"Beneath that rock, to the King's surprise and delight, there lay a small boy whose skin gleamed like gold. Because of this, and because of the fact that he had been lying under a stone, the King called the child 'Kim Nee Wa,' or 'Golden Toad.' And he cherished this son whom Heaven had sent him in such a strange way.

"Now it was this same Kim Nee Wa who succeeded his father on the throne of that northern kingdom. And it was in his courts one day that a marvelous happening occurred. One of his wives, sitting by a little stream in the garden, saw a tiny white cloud moving toward her. Gently it floated inside her dress, where it turned into an egg.

"When the cloud egg was hatched and a fine baby boy was presented to the King, he grew very angry. 'This child is surely the son of a demon!' he cried. 'Throw it among the pigs.'

"But the fierce boars did not harm the child. They grew gentle as cooing doves, and they blew their warm breath on the baby so that the night air should not harm him.

" 'Throw the demon child to the hunting dogs,' the angry King cried. But again snarling beasts became quiet. The dogs licked the face and hands of the tiny boy and warmed him with their breath.

" 'Put him amid the wild horses,' ordered the King, for he feared this strange child. The wild horses also breathed softly upon the boy, and the mares fed him with their warm milk.

" '*Ai*, it is the will of the Jade Emperor of Heaven that this boy shall live,' the King finally gave in. 'His mother shall bring the child up as our son.'

"All marveled at the beauty and cleverness of the boy. From his shining face people called him 'Child of the Sun' or 'Brightness of the Morning,' which are just ways of saying 'Light of the East.' Always kind to animals, he had a special gift for handling the horses in the King's stables, and he was made master there.

"But, above all, people wondered at the boy's skill with the bow and arrow. At your age, Yong Tu, he could bring down a flying swallow. At fifteen he could slay a swift-running deer or pierce the eye of a wild goose flying high in the clouds. His like was not known on all the eight coasts. More often he was called 'Chu Mong,' or 'Skillful Archer.'

"Splendid and handsome, kind and skillful, he was. All

in that kingdom preferred Chu Mong above any of the other sons of the King. Only his jealous brothers disliked him.

"One day Chu Mong learned from his mother of a plot they were making to put him to death.

"'You must flee, Skillful Archer. You must flee this night, my dear son,' she warned.

"With loyal friends at his side Chu Mong slipped secretly out of the palace. Under the light of the amber moon they galloped away south. When the morning sun gilded the peaks of the Ever-White Mountains, they were stopped by the deep duck-green waters of the River Apnok. They halted in dismay, for they could hear the sounds of the galloping horses of the pursuers.

"'Hark, my friends!' said the Archer. 'Listen well! Do you hear? My brothers are coming. They are very near. I will call on the river dragon to help me.' And drawing his bow he shot three of his arrows into the stream.

"Straightway, my children, the river waters became black instead of duck-green. It was black with the backs of ten thousand fish. Squeezed tightly together, the fish made a firm bridge, over which Chu Mong and his companions easily crossed to the opposite bank. When the King's sons galloped up, the bridge of fish had once more floated apart, and Skillful Archer was safe.

"Traveling on to the south, Chu Mong met friendly people. Three attached themselves to him to act as his guides. One wore the garments of the fishermen of this new land. A second was dressed like its farmers, or workers with tools. A third was clad in the embroidered robes of the officials. All welcomed Chu Mong and made him their king.

"Many fleet horsemen and many skillful archers were trained in the kingdom of this Chu Mong. Some say it was he who invented the topknot, and who taught our people to eat politely with bowls, spoons, and chopsticks.

"In his kingdom all lived in kindness and peace, and its ruler's fame spread abroad. Many years later to honor Chu Mong, so the tale says, men gave his name, 'Light of the East,' to the whole country. They called it 'Chosun,' which is to say, 'Land of Morning Brightness.'"

KI JA'S

POTTERY

HATS

ONE afternoon, not long after the Ancestors' Feast, Halmoni and Ok Cha and the others in the Inner Court were startled by a great noise beyond the Middle Gate. The cries and shouts there brought the women out upon the little verandas and sent the small boys running into the Outer Court to see what was the matter.

"It was a fight, Halmoni," Yong Tu reported, coming back, breathless. "A fight between So, the stableboy, and that peddler robber who carried away one of the saddles the last time he came inside our gates. You should have seen them, Ok Cha. Each grabbed the other one by the topknot, and they would not let go. Oh, they were rolling about on the ground in the dust. But the peddler was getting the worst of the fight. It was Uncle Chong Yang who stopped them at last."

"There are far too many fights," Halmoni said, shaking her old head in disgust. "Our Emperor will have to bring back again pottery hats, like those of Ki Ja."

"Pottery hats, Halmoni?" Yong Tu asked, dropping down on the veranda step by his grandmother. He was still out of breath. Besides, he thought these curious words might mean a story.

"Wouldn't pottery hats break?" Ok Cha put in.

"*Yé*, blessed girl, that is why it was decreed that all in the kingdom should wear them. I think it was when Ki Ja was emperor. Or it may have been during the rule of one of his forty descendants. At any rate, it was long ago when men were even rougher than they are today. In those days they were constantly fighting, pulling one another hither and yon by their topknots. Neighbor fought with neighbor. Band fought against band. Men swung their clubs if only to battle with a mosquito. It was not safe to walk abroad on city street or country road.

"So Ki Ja sent forth the order that every man must wear a broad pottery hat, made of baked clay. Two feet across it must be, and shaped like a mushroom so that it came well down over his ears. There was a reason for that too, but I'll speak of it later.

"On a light framework of straw the wet clay was spread smooth. Then the hat was put into a hot oven to bake hard, just like the porcelain bowls in our kitchen. Of course the pottery hats broke easily, as Ok Cha has guessed. The

Yong Tu admired the tall hats, made of fine horsehair, which his father and uncles wore inside as well as outside the house.

slightest jar would send them flying off into the road where they would lie, broken in pieces. How could men fight with such hats on their heads?"

"They might have taken them off," Yong Tu said practically.

"No, clever boy, that was against the law," Halmoni replied, smiling. "A pottery hat cost a very large sum to buy, but it cost a larger sum to lose one or break one. A man must not only pay a big fine but also go to prison and be well paddled if he broke his precious hat.

"The Emperor's scheme worked very well. With his topknot hidden safely under the great hat, and not daring to step outside his own courts without one, a man had no chance of taking part in a fight. Ki Ja's pottery hats brought peace once again to this unruly land."

"And the shape of the hats, Halmoni," Ok Cha reminded her grandmother.

"*Hé*, that was good, too. The great round hats were shaped like a dome, like the mourner's hat Neighbor Yi has been wearing ever since his father rode the dragon to Heaven last year. So big they were that men could not come close enough to one another's ears to whisper in secret. The Emperor knew of plots being hatched to cause him much trouble. With such pottery hats he could be sure that his spies would hear all that went on.

"The people did not like these great burdensome hats, and they wanted to make them smaller," the old woman continued. "Yet I know one tale of how his great hat saved the life of a man. It happened in early spring when the river was still covered with its winter cloak of ice. A man walking across the ice stepped upon a thin place and fell through into the water. He would have drowned if his broad hat had not caught on the edges of the hole.

"Crowds gathered on the bank like ants running to feast on a fishbone. The man's son wrung his hands. He had started forward to pull his father out by his hat. But the village elder cried, 'Wait! Do not tug at his hat. His chin strap will break and he surely will drown.'

"The wise old man told the son to break through the crown of the big pottery hat so that he could grasp his father's topknot. Standing up stiff like a horn, it made an excellent handle. With a firm grip on the topknot the son was able to pull his father safely up out of the water."

"What happened to all those pottery hats, Halmoni?" Yong Tu asked when the old woman paused for a breath.

"*Ai,* they were probably broken at last, or else turned upside down and used for storing rice or soybeans. To please their customers, the hatmakers first left off the clay covering upon the straw framework. Then they made the hats smaller and smaller, and lighter and lighter. And since men had by that time learned to live without fighting, the Emperor's pottery hat decree was withdrawn.

"But even today our men's hats are designed chiefly to protect and cover up their precious topknots. That is why they wear hats inside, as well as outside, their own houses. So's topknot-pulling with the dishonest peddler shows what happens to persons who go about without hats."

Yong Tu admired above everything the tall black hats made of fine horsehair gauze, which were worn by his father and his uncles. He liked to lift them, because he never could believe hats could be so light. "They're no heavier than feathers," he used to say to Ok Cha. Indeed their father's hat weighed only a little more than an ounce.

On cloudy days the boy was often sent to fetch the rain cover for his father's horsehair hat. The slightest dampness would melt the stiffening of its crown which stood up so proudly. An oiled-paper pleated covering, shaped like a tiny tent, was kept tucked inside Kim Hong Chip's sleeve, whence it could be quickly pulled out when the rain came.

Yong Tu admired also the neat gauze skullcap his father wore under the hat, with his fine upstanding topknot rising through the hole in its top. Like most *yangbans*, Kim Hong Chip sometimes put a small silver pin in his topknot. That was to drive away evil spirits which might wish to grab it. Other times he wore in it a button of jade, amber, or turquoise.

The amber beads on the chin strap that held his hat firmly upon his dignified head were a sign of this man's importance. More ordinary men had only a narrow black ribbon tied under their chins.

Yong Tu never thought it strange that a boy of ten years, like himself, should wear a long braid down his back, like a girl. It never occurred to him to wonder why his father and his uncles should bother with long hair, which had to be combed and oiled with such care.

This boy looked forward to the time when he, too, would be old enough to marry and put his hair up in the honorable topknot. That would be a great day, a lucky day chosen by the soothsayer. All the family would gather in the Hall of Ceremonies. Kim Hong Chip, as Master of the House, would unbraid his son's long hair. He would then comb it upward, giving it a firm twist and tying it tightly with string. The horsehair cap would be put on, and in his new long white coat, Yong Tu would bow before the tablets of the Ancestors. Then they, too, would know that he had become a man. There would be feasts for the Ancestors and for the family and friends who came to congratulate him.

If anyone had asked Yong Tu why a topknot was so important, he would have just looked surprised and would have answered, "It is the custom." That was reason enough in this land of Korea where people had followed the ways of their ancestors for more than four thousand years.

WHY THE DOG

AND

THE CAT

ARE

NOT FRIENDS

ONE warm autumn afternoon sounds of barking from the Outer Court drifted to the veranda where Ok Cha was helping her grandmother sort pine seeds for the New Year cakes.

"I have a riddle for you, Halmoni," the little girl said.

"My ears are open, Jade Child," the old woman replied, smiling fondly down upon her favorite granddaughter.

"Here it is then. Who in this house first goes forth to welcome the coming guest?"

"Would it be your father, the Master of our House?" Halmoni asked thoughtfully, pretending she had never heard this old riddle before.

"No, Halmoni, it would not be Abuji. The Master of this House greets his guests only when they have entered the Outer Court." Ok Cha was delighted because her grandmother did not guess the answer at once.

"Would it be Pak, the gatekeeper?" Halmoni asked, wrinkling her smooth, old, ivory-colored brow, as if she were puzzled.

"Oh no, Halmoni. Shall I tell you? Well, it is Dog!"

"To be sure it is Dog." The Korean grandmother nodded

her dark head. "Dog is the true gatekeeper of our house."

Most of the day, and even at night, this shaggy shepherd, which everyone inside the Kim courts called "Dog," lay half way through the doghole cut in the bottom of the bamboo gate. With his head thrust through the opening, he was the first to see and give warning of approaching visitors.

Dog took his duties as gatekeeper much more seriously than old Pak, who slept most of the time in the door of the servants' houses just inside the gate. Of course, now and then he went out into the street to hunt bits of food that might have been thrown out there by the neighbors. Or he sometimes left his post to bark at a bird or to chase a stray cat.

It was this last pastime that brought Dog now racing through the Middle Gate and into the Inner Court. Around the tall pottery water jars went the black cat with the brown dog at her tail. Over and under the seesaw they flew, and into the corner where Yong Tu and his cousins were busy making kites for the New Year flying.

"*Wori! Wori!* Dog, come here," Yong Tu called severely. And the boy joined in the chase, finally catching the excited dog by the neck and holding him tight until the black cat got away to safety in the Garden of Green Gems, beyond the women's houses.

These children did not have much sympathy for the cat, but Yong Tu was afraid the animals might spoil his precious kite-making materials which were spread out on the ground. The Kims liked Dog because he was such a good watchman. But he was in no way an indoor pet like the dogs of Western lands. This black cat, which often

crept over their wall, was very wild. Once Ok Cha had tried
to pet it, but the cat would only growl, spit at her, and
scratch.

"Why do dogs and cats fight so, Halmoni?" the little
girl asked, looking up from her tray of pine seeds.

"My grandmother used to tell me a story about that,"
Halmoni said. "And I'll tell it to you." Somehow Yong Tu
and his cousins must have guessed their grandmother was
beginning a story. Before she was well started, they had
brought their papers, their bamboo sticks, and their glue-
pots and set up their little kite factory at her feet.

"The dog and the cat in my tale lived in a small wineshop on the bank of a broad river beside a ferry, my children. Old Koo, the shopkeeper, had neither wife nor child.
In his little hut he lived by himself except for this dog and
this cat. The tame beasts never left his side. While he sold
wine in the shop, the dog kept guard at the door and the
cat caught mice in the storeroom. When he walked on the
river bank, they trotted by his side. When he lay down to
sleep upon the warm floor, they crept close to his back.
They were good enough friends then, the dog and the cat,
but that was before the disaster occurred and the cat be-
haved so badly.

"Old Koo was poor, but he was honest and kind. His
shop was not like those where travelers are persuaded to
drink wine until they become drunk and roll on the ground.
Only one kind of wine was sold, but it was a good wine.
Once they had tasted it, Koo's customers came back again
and again to fill their long-necked wine bottles.

" 'Where does Old Koo get so much wine?' the neighbors
used to ask one another. 'No new jars are ever delivered by

bull carts at his door. He makes no wine himself, yet his black jug is never without wine to pour for his customers.'

"No one knew the answer to the riddle save Old Koo himself, and he told it to no one except his dog and his cat. Years before he opened his wineshop, Koo had worked on the ferry. One cold rainy night when the last ferry had returned, a strange traveler came to the gate of his hut.

" 'Honorable Sir, he begged Koo, 'give me a drop of good wine to drive out the damp chill.'

" 'My wine jug is almost empty,' Koo told the traveler. 'I have only a little for my evening drink, but no doubt you need the wine far more than I. I'll share it with you.' And he filled up a bowl for his strange, thirsty guest.

"The stranger on leaving put into the ferryman's hand a bit of bright golden amber. 'Keep this in your wine jug,' he said, 'and it will always be full.'

"Now, as Old Koo told his dog and his cat, that traveler must have been a spirit from Heaven, for when Koo lifted the black jug, it was heavy with wine. When he filled his bowl from it, he thought he had never tasted a drink so sweet and so rich. No matter how much he poured, the wine in the jug never grew less.

"Here was a treasure indeed. With a jug that never ran dry, he could open a wineshop. He would no longer have to go back and forth, back and forth, in the ferryboat over the river in all kinds of weather.

"All went well until one day when he was serving a traveler, Koo found to his horror that his black jug was empty. He shook it and shook it, but no answering tinkle came from the hard amber charm that should have been inside.

" '*Ai-go! Ai-go!*' Koo wailed. 'I must unknowingly have poured the amber out into the bottle of one of my customers. *Ai-go!* What shall I do?'

"The dog and the cat shared their master's sadness. The dog howled at the moon, and the cat prowled around the shop, sniffing and sniffing under the rice jars and even high up on the rafters. These animals knew the secret of the magic wine jug, for the old man had often talked to them about the stranger's amber charm.

" 'I am sure I could find the charm,' the cat said to the dog, 'if I only could catch its amber smell.'

" 'We shall search for it together,' the dog suggested. 'We shall go through every house in the neighborhood. When you sniff it out, I will run home with it.'

"So they began their quest. They asked all the cats and dogs they met for news of the lost amber. They prowled about all the houses, but not a trace could they find of their master's magic charm.

" 'We must try the other side of the river,' the dog said at last. 'They will not let us ride across on the ferryboat. But when the winter cold comes and the river's stomach is solid, we can safely creep over the ice, like everyone else.'

"Thus it was that one winter morning the dog and the cat crossed the river to the opposite side. As soon as the owners were not looking, they crept into the houses. The dog sniffed round the courtyards, and the cat even climbed up on the beams under the sloping grass roofs. Day after day, week after week, month after month, they searched and they searched, but with no success.

"Spring was at hand. The joyful fish in the river were bumping their backs against the soft ice. At last, one day, high up on the top of a great brassbound chest, the cat smelled the amber. But, *ai*, the welcome perfume came from inside a tightly closed box. What could they do? If they pushed the box off the chest and let it break on the floor, the Master of the House would surely be warned and chase them away.

" 'We must get help from the rats,' the clever dog cried. 'They can gnaw a hole in the box for us and get the amber out. In return, we can promise to let them live in peace for ten years.' This plan was all against the nature of a cat, but this one loved its master and it consented.

"The rats consented, too. It seemed to them almost too good to be true that both the cats and the dogs might leave them alone for ten whole peaceful years. It took the rats many days to gnaw a hole in that box, but at last it was done. The cat tried to get at the amber with its soft paw, but the hole was too small. Finally a young mouse had to be sent in through the wee hole. It succeeded in pulling the amber out with its teeth.

" 'How pleased our master will be! Now good luck will live again under his roof,' the cat and the dog said to each other. In their joy at finding the lost amber charm, they ran around and around as if they were having fits.

" 'But how shall we get the amber back to the other side of the river?' the cat cried in dismay. 'You know I cannot swim.'

" 'You shall hold the amber safely inside your mouth, Cat,' the dog replied wisely. 'You shall climb on my back, and I'll swim you over the river.'

"And so it happened. Clawing the thick shaggy hair of the dog's back, the cat kept its balance until they had almost reached their own bank of the stream. But there, playing along the shore, were a number of children, who burst into laughter when they saw the strange ferryman and his curious passenger. 'A cat riding on the back of a dog! Ho! Ho! Ho!' they laughed. 'Ha! Ha! Ha! Ho! Ho! Ho! Just look at that.' They called to their parents, and they came to laugh, too.

"Now the faithful dog paid no attention to their foolish mirth, but the cat could not help joining them in the fun. It, too, began to laugh, and from its open mouth Old Koo's precious amber charm dropped down upon the river bottom.

"The dog shook the cat off his back, he was so angry, and it was a miracle that the creature at last got safely to the shore. In a rage the dog chased the cat, which finally took refuge in the crotch of a tree. There the cat shook the moisture out of its fur. By spitting and spitting, it got rid of the water it had swallowed while in the river. The cat dared not come down out of the tree until the angry dog had gone away.

"That, so my grandmother said, is why the dog and the cat are never friends, my dear ones. That is why, too, a cat always spits when a strange dog comes too near. That is why a cat does not like to get its feet wet."

"But what about the amber charm and poor Old Koo?" Ok Cha asked anxiously.

"It was that dog who finally saved the fortunes of the old wineshop keeper," Halmoni explained. "First, he tried swimming out into the stream to look for the amber. But it was too deep for him to see the bottom. Then he sat beside the river fishermen, wishing he had a line or a net like theirs that would bring up the golden prize he sought. Suddenly from a fish that had just been pulled out of the water, the dog sniffed amber perfume. Grabbing that fish up in his mouth before the fisherman could stop him, he galloped off home.

" 'Well done, Dog,' said Old Koo. 'There is only a little food left under our roof. This fish will make a good meal for you and me.' The old man cut open the fish and, to his surprise and delight, the bit of amber rolled out.

" 'Now I can put my magic charm back into the jug,' Koo said to himself. 'But there must be at least a little wine in it to start the jug flowing again. While I go out to buy some, I'll just lock the amber up inside my clothes chest.'

"When Koo came back with the wine and opened the chest, he found that instead of the one suit he had stored in it, there were now two. Where his last string of cash had been, there were two strings. And he guessed that the secret of this amber charm was that it would double whatever it touched.

"With this knowledge Koo became rich beyond telling. And in the gate of his fine new house he cut a doghole for his faithful friend, who had saved him from starving. There, day and night, like our own four-footed gate guard, the fat dog lay watching in peace and well-fed contentment. But all through his life he never again killed a mouse nor made a friend of a cat."

STICKS

AND

TURNIPS!

STICKS

AND

TURNIPS!

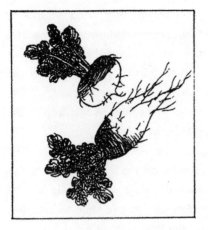

IT WAS *kimchee* time once again. In the courtyard the
crisp, cool autumn air was heavy with the savory smell
of this good cabbage pickle, which every Korean liked
so well to eat with his rice.

When each little eating table was prepared in the
kitchens of the Kims and their neighbors, the main bowl
upon it was heaped high with fluffy, steaming hot rice.
In the other bowls ringed about this one, there might
sometimes be soy sauce or bean soup, sometimes seaweed
cooked in oil, sometimes dried salted fish, or even meat
stew. But there was always one bowl filled with spicy
kimchee.

Now, at *kimchee* time the courtyards of the Kims were
carpeted with long, thin heads of Chinese cabbage. West-
erners call this celery cabbage because of its white stalks
topped with pale green. Huge piles of turnips and onions,
strings of garlic and ginger, and bundles of strong salt fish
also were there.

Ok Cha and the other little girls of the household tagged

behind their grandmother while she supervised the women who were washing and soaking the vegetables in salt water. The children liked to peer over the rim of the great *kimchee* jars to see how nearly full they were. It was dark on the bottoms of the jars, a full six feet below the level of the courtyard. Like the water jars, they were sunk deep in the earth to keep them from freezing.

"*Ai*, take care, Ok Cha! You are not a red pepper. Nor yet a fat turnip to be mixed with the *kimchee!*" Halmoni cried out, seizing the rosy red skirt of the child as she almost lost her balance. She was just in time to save her from a headlong dive into the huge pottery pit.

The old woman led the little girl away to safety on the other side of the courtyard, where Yong Tu and his cousins were carving giant turnips into little round lanterns. The boys had beside them slender rods cut from the bamboo in the Garden of Green Gems. On these little sticks they hung their turnip lanterns, when they had pasted bits of kite paper over the holes dug in their sides.

The Korean grandmother was tired. She was glad to sit down on the nearest veranda step and watch her grandsons at their work.

"Sticks and turnips! Sticks and turnips!" the old woman murmured, shaking her head solemnly, but with a twinkle in her dark eyes. "Take care, my sons. Take care you don't turn someone into an ox."

"Turn someone into an ox, Halmoni?" Yong Tu asked, wondering. "How could that be? And what have sticks and turnips to do with such a strange happening?"

"It's an old tale about a farmer, blessed boy," Halmoni replied. "A farmer who took revenge on a city official who tricked him. It all happened long, long ago. Who can tell whether it really happened at all? But the tale goes like this——

"There was a farmer named Cho who had had years of good luck in his rice fields. Such good luck was his that he had many huge chests filled with long strings of cash. But like many another fortunate man, he was not content with his lot. Cho grew tired of plowing his fields and harvesting the good rice. He longed for the softer, easier life of the capital city of Seoul."

" 'Now if I could only buy for myself an official's hat, I could grow even richer,' Cho said to his family. Then, as now, my children, it was always the government officials who grew rich. They handled the money the people paid in taxes into the King's treasury. Of course a good deal of that money went into their own brassbound chests. They called this their rightful 'squeeze.'

"*Hué*, that farmer came up to Seoul. He straightway sought out the Prime Minister to ask for a good position at the King's court. Cho made the Minister many rich presents. He went every day to the Minister's courtyard to plead his case.

" 'Perhaps tomorrow,' the Minister said every time Cho laid a gift at his feet. But that tomorrow never came. One year—two years—three years—and four. Again and again, Cho sent home for more money out of his cash chests. One does not eat for nothing here in the capital.

"Then one day there came word that his cash chests were all empty. His rice fields were neglected. His house would have to be sold. His family were starving.

" 'Help me to the position now, Honorable Sir,' Cho

pleaded with the Minister. 'My cash chests are empty. I shall have to give up and go home.'

"But the Minister only shook his head and again said, 'Perhaps tomorrow.'

"Cho turned away from that Minister with rage in his heart. He vowed he'd get even somehow and sometime.

"On his journey home Cho took shelter one night under the grass roof of an old country couple. They made him welcome. They shared their rice and their *kimchee* with him. They gave him the warmest part of the floor to sleep upon. But as the sun rose and the cock crew, Cho, half-awake, heard them talking above him.

" 'It is now time to take the ox to the market,' the old man said to his wife. 'Get me the halter.' And he began to tap Cho lightly all over his body with four little sticks. Cho tried to cry out, but to his surprise the only noise he could make was the bellow of an ox. When he rose from the floor, he found himself standing on all fours, and the old woman was putting a ring in his nose. As he went out of the hut, he had to take care lest his horns catch in the door-posts. The poor man had been turned into a great hairy ox.

"As he was led along the highway by the ring in his nose, Cho's heart was filled with dismay at the trick that had been played upon him. He was the finest and fattest among the many animals at the cattle market, but his owner asked such a high price that at first none could buy. Finally there came a butcher who had tarried too long in a wineshop. His senses were dull, and he paid the high price. Then he led poor Cho away to be killed.

"Fortunately for Cho, the road they took passed another wineshop. There the drunken butcher tied his prize ox to a stake, so that he might go in and have just one more bowl of *sool*.

"Cho himself was hungry, and thirsty, too. And just across the road from the wineshop there was a field of fine turnips. With his great strength the ox-man was able to pull the stake out of the ground and to break his way through the roadside hedge. He pulled up a juicy turnip and sank his teeth into it.

"As he munched, Cho's hairy hide began to itch. His great body began to shake. He rose up on his hind legs. When he looked down at his hands and feet, he saw to his delight that he was a man again. Cho walked out into the road, where he met the drunken butcher, who begged him to tell him if he had seen his lost ox.

"As Cho turned his face again towards home, he said to himself, 'Sticks and turnips! Sticks and turnips! That is the secret. And if I can just get hold of those magic sticks, I can take my revenge upon that selfish Prime Minister.'

"Going back to the hut of the old country couple, he was welcomed as before. But this time, as soon as they were asleep, he began his search for the four magic sticks. Long before the sun rose and the cock crew, Cho crept out of the house with the sticks hidden in his sleeve. All the way back to Seoul, lest he should forget, he kept saying to himself over and over again, 'Sticks and turnips! Sticks and turnips! That is the secret.'"

"Now Cho knew well the sleeping room of the official. The gates were unlocked, and the doors stood wide open. In the bright moonlight he had no trouble at all in creeping in to his victim.

"With two of the little sticks he began to tap the sleeping Prime Minister. With wicked delight he watched the man's hands turn into hoofs and horns sprout from his forehead. But the Minister began to stir before Cho could use the other two sticks on his legs. He had to hurry away with his task only half done.

"When the moon gave place to the sun in the heavens, there was panic in the Minister's household. 'Our Master can only bellow like an ox. There are horns on his head and hoofs where his hands should be. His head and his shoulders are covered with ox hide.' This awful news spread over the countryside like leaves in an autumn wind.

"The servants ran forth to summon a famous doctor. He came in his fine chair, borne on the shoulders of four men. But he could do nothing for the bewitched Minister.

"They next sent for a sorceress, the most famous *mudang* in all the city. Out at the grave of the Minister's ancestors she wailed and she howled, she danced and she rolled about on the ground. She prayed and she prayed, but no help came to the Minister, who now was half ox.

"It was then that the rice farmer Cho arrived once again at the Prime Minister's gate. He pretended to be surprised and shocked when he heard of the great man's curious plight.

" 'I can cure the Great Man,' he said to the Prime Minister when the family led him in to see the ox-man. 'We had a case once like yours in my village. I surely can cure you, but the price is the position for which I have begged you so long.'

"The ox-man bellowed consent, and the family promised that whatever Cho asked should be given him. Then the rice farmer went out to the market. He bought several turnips, which he dried in an oven until they could be ground to a powder. Everyone gathered to watch the Prime Minister lap up the turnip 'medicine' with his great ox's tongue. There were cries of delight when the horns and the hoofs grew smaller and smaller. Together with the ox head and hide, they soon disappeared.

"As soon as the Prime Minister was restored to his former self, he brought forth many strings of cash for his savior. Cho was given an important position at the court. He was granted the right to wear an official's hat with a jade button in his topknot. An official's gown, embroidered with the golden dragon, was brought for him. A tiger's skin covered the roof of his sedan chair. Fame and fortune were his, and all because of his finding the curious secret of the magic 'Sticks and turnips!' "

THE

TIGER

AND

THE

PUPPY

THAT hole in our gate is a very good thing, Halmoni," Yong Tu said when his grandmother had finished her tale. "It lets Dog pass through, but it keeps bad people out."

"Yé, Dragon Head," the old woman replied. "And it's too small for a tiger. That's what the puppy found out. By means of the doghole he saved his village when all the wise men and all the brave hunters had failed."

The children moved closer to their grandmother. Here was a new story about a tiger. There was nothing that made the shivers go up and down their backs so delightfully as tales about this mighty King of the Mountains.

Korean tigers are larger than their brothers in warmer countries. The soft fur of their tawny coats is thicker and longer, so as to protect them from the sharp winter cold of the high mountain sides on which they live.

Especially in the north, in those times, these huge yellow-and-black beasts were the terror of the countrysides. In the summer they fed upon the mountain deer and the little sucklings of the wild boar. But when the winter came and game was scarce in those rocky hills, the tigers crept down into the valleys. They prowled through the villages and even crept into the cities. Yong Tu and Ok Cha could themselves remember when a tiger once made its way into the very courtyards of the Emperor's palace in Seoul.

"To this village in the north," Halmoni began her story, "there came one winter a great tiger, far bigger than any those people ever had seen. Strong was this beast, strong enough to carry off a grown man. And carry off a man it did, a man who was foolish enough to go out on the village street after night had fallen. Cows were not safe from that tiger, and pigs disappeared unless they were shut up tight inside the strong walls of the village courtyards.

" 'We must set traps for Mountain Uncle,' said the head official of the village. And they dug a pit at each end of the village street. Over these deep yawning holes they laid small logs and branches. They covered them lightly with earth and leaves, to deceive the great beast. When he walked across them, he would surely fall in.

"But the tiger seemed to know about the hidden traps. He did not walk across them. Even when they were baited with live pigs, he did not go near them. Yet the village people could tell that he still came. The head official himself was frightened almost out of his wits by the sound of that tiger clawing away at the grass thatch on his roof. Only by good luck and by shouting, and by beating on brass pots, did he succeed in driving the great beast away.

" 'We must call out the hunters from all the countryside,' the village people said next. The tiger hunters came, in their blue uniforms and their red-tasseled hats. Their matchlock guns were slung over their shoulders. Their deer-horn cases were filled with bullets, and their oilpaper packets of gunpowder were safe and dry inside their sleeves. They did not forget to wind around their arms the long cords which could be fired to set the guns off. Walking swiftly and softly on their straw sandals, they started out for the hills.

"The village official saw the hunters depart with relief," the Korean grandmother continued. "Surely such a band of strong brave men would find the tiger. They would beat about in the bushes until he came forth. They would wound him with their guns and finish him off with their spears. Then his precious soft skin would be the prize of the village official himself. The hunters could have the tiger meat to eat. He might also let them have the bones, teeth, and claws to sell to the medicine makers."

In Korea, in those times, powders made of tiger bones, tiger teeth, and tiger claws were highly prized. The ancient warriors swallowed these medicines to give them strength and courage such as only a tiger possesses. Halmoni herself always took a tiger-bone tonic in the spring when she felt weak and tired.

"Did the hunters catch the tiger, Halmoni?" Ok Cha said, almost holding her breath in excitement.

"No, baby dear, they came back empty-handed. Perhaps it was because the beaters were afraid to go into the deepest parts of the forest. Or perhaps Old Mountain Uncle was once more too smart for them.

" 'Let us put a new picture of Honorable White Whiskers in the spirit shrine outside the village,' the people said. 'Let us call on the spirit of Tu-ee, that great enemy of the tiger. He will help us drive him away.'

"That night, at the slightest sound, the villagers would run out into their courtyards, crying, 'Tu-ee is coming! Tu-ee! Tu-ee!' But the bloody feathers of some chickens that had strayed out of their courtyard showed that the King of the Mountains had been there once again, in spite of their calling upon his spirit foe.

"So frightened of the dreaded tiger were the people of the village that they all hid inside their houses at night. They shut up their animals, and when the yellow and black beast stalked down the road, not a living creature was to be seen. Not one, that is, until on a certain night a foolish puppy left the side of its mother inside the stable and crept out to the gate.

"It was winter, and the great tiger was hungry. When he saw the head of the little dog thrust through the gate hole, the beast licked its chops. With a bound he made for the hole, but it was, of course, far too small for him to force his huge body through.

"Ordinarily, a tiger would not have bothered with a morsel so small as this puppy. Nothing less than a cow or a pig or a man would have attracted his notice. But the village folk had been so watchful that he had had no food in days, and his stomach was empty.

"Lashing his great tail and snarling deep down in his throat, he fixed his flaming eyes on the mud wall before him, beyond which his prey lay. The mud wall was high, and there were sharp, jagged rocks along its top. But the tiger thought he could leap it. Gathering his strength, he made one mighty bound. And over he went.

"But no puppy was there. With a sharp yip of terror the little dog had run out through the gate hole into the street. The tiger could only see the tip of his tail.

"There was nothing for Mountain Uncle to do but to leap over the wall after him. With another great effort the yellow-and-black tiger made the high jump. But, of course, this time again he found no puppy there. The little fellow had wisely run back inside the gate."

The children laughed in delight at the picture their grandmother painted of the tiger leaping back and forth, back and forth, and of the puppy running in and out, in and out, of the gate hole.

"That was good, Halmoni," Yong Tu cried.

"And what finally happened?" Ok Cha asked eagerly.

"What finally happened? Well, as you all know, there is no braver beast than a fierce tiger, nor one more stubborn. But the tiger's great head can hold only a single idea at a time, and this beast thought of nothing but of his own hunger. Over and over the high wall he leaped, over and over, until at last his strong heart gave out. And that's how it was, so this story goes, that next morning the villagers found the tiger lying dead outside in the street, and the little puppy fast asleep in the hole in the gate.

"Half the year the Koreans hunt the tiger, and half the year the tiger hunts the Koreans, so the Chinese say," Halmoni told her grandchildren. "When a tiger kills one of our hunters, the man's soul becomes the slave of the beast. His spirit is forced to take on again his human form. He walks along the mountain path and lures other hunters into the thickets where the tiger can kill them. Only when a second man is eaten by the tiger, may the soul of the first one go freely up to the Heavenly Kingdom."

This Korean grandmother remembered tales of men who turned into tigers and of tigers which turned into men. In all the tales the tiger was strong and the tiger was brave. That is why on the Korean flags of those times there was often a tiger with a flaming tongue, or with a firebrand in his claw. That is why tiger heads were embroidered on the caps of the palace guards. That is why, too, these leaping beasts were shown in the designs on embroidered screens and inlaid chests of *yangban* homes like the Kims'.

But in most of Halmoni's stories, also, the tiger was shown to be far less wise than he was strong. That is the reason, so this Korean grandmother said, why a weak little puppy was able to get the best of the mighty King of the Mountains.

Ancient Korean warriors swallowed medicines made of powdered tiger bones to give them more courage and strength.

THE BIRD

OF

THE FIVE

VIRTUES

ONE day late in the autumn a farmer caught a wild goose," Halmoni said to her grandson Yong Tu. "I tell you about that goose, blessed boy, because it will help you remember your lesson."

The boy was sitting with his feet tucked under him on the warm floor of his grandmother's apartment. In his hands was a book whose Korean name meant "A Primer for the Young." Over and over, half aloud, he had been repeating the words "*In-eui-ye-chi-shin.*" As he said them, they were all run together like one very long word. But they meant five different things: love, right behavior, good form, wisdom, and faith. These were the five virtues which every Korean child was taught to remember.

At his grandmother's words Yong Tu put his primer aside. Her story would be far more interesting, he knew, than the lessons in his book.

"Well, this farmer caught the wild goose. He clipped off its wings so that it could not fly away with the other birds, to the south. Thinking to gain favor, he made a present of that wild goose to the Governor of his province. The Governor was indeed pleased. He put the goose in his garden, and his servants fed it good grain.

"One day as the Governor walked in his garden, a servant addressed him. 'Honorable Sir,' he said, bowing low, 'that fat wild goose would make a very fine feast. Its flesh is sweet and tender. Its flavor is fine. I pray you, kill it and eat it.'

" 'Kill a wild goose and eat it?' the good Governor replied. 'That I will not. The wild goose is the bird of all the Five Virtues, *In-eui-ye-chi-shin*.'

" 'How could that be, Honorable Scholar?' the servant asked. 'How could a bird know about the Five Virtues?'

" 'Think, Man!' the Governor said. 'First, the wild goose is an example of love. It does not fight like the eagle nor hunt like the falcon. It lives in peace and friendship with its fellows. Second, the wild goose is a bird of excellent behavior. When it takes a mate, it observes all the rules of right living. And when its mate dies, the goose mourns her loss like a true wife. She comes back again and again to her former nesting place, alone and a widow. What wedding in our land is complete without the wild goose as a symbol of wifely devotion?

" 'No, my good man, I should not wish to kill a bird with such a fine character. Watch the wild geese, how they fly. In order, and with ceremony, they make their procession across the blue sky. And what wisdom they show, seeking the warmth of the south in the cold winter and the cool air of the north when the hot summer comes!

" 'You have seen for yourself, how they come back to

our north country every year at the same time. Thus they keep the faith. *Ai*, the wild goose lives by the Five Virtues. Who would destroy so noble a bird?'

"Read the Five Laws to me from your primer, my young schoolman," the Korean Grandmother said when her little story of the wild goose came to its end.

"Amid heaven and earth," Yong Tu repeated in the singsong voice he always used in studying his lessons, "man is the noblest being. And man is noble chiefly because he follows the Five Laws. As the wise Mencius said,

" 'There should be between father and son proper relationship, with love from the father and duty from the son;

" 'Between king and his courtiers there should be right dealing, the king being correct and the courtier being loyal;

" 'Between husband and wife, there should be kindness and obedience;

" 'Between old and young there should be consideration and respect; and

" 'Between friend and friend, there should be faith that is kept.' "

The boy drew a long breath. He had learned his lesson well, and he did not forget to add, "If man does not follow these laws, he is no better than the beasts."

THE

BLIND

MAN'S

DAUGHTER

Sim Chung's face was as smooth as a piece of ivory carving.
Her brows had the curves of a butterfly's wings.

T HOSE words are as precious as clearest green jade, Yong Tu," Halmoni declared when her grandson had ceased reciting the Five Laws of Behavior. "But most precious of all are those that tell of the duty of a child to his parents. Obedience in all things, respect for the aged—those are the most important, and the ones which bring great rewards. Have I ever told you the story of Chung, the dutiful daughter of Sim, the blind beggar?

"Well, it happened five hundred years ago, perhaps even more. In a certain village there lived this good girl whose name was Sim Chung. Her mother was dead, and her father was growing blind. Chung was the one treasure of that poor man. Her face was smooth and white, like a piece of ivory carving. Her brows had the curves of a butterfly's wings, and her hair shone like the lacquer on the shining black table in Ancestors' House. In all her life no illness had ever befallen Chung. Not even the Great Spirit of Smallpox had been able to harm her.

"Chung was as good and kind as she was fair and wise. She wasted no grain of rice nor drop of *kimchee*. She guided her father's faltering steps, but with his blindness the poor man no longer could work. Their possessions had to be sold, one after another, to keep them alive.

"When the girl was grown up, it was no longer proper that she go out on the street with her old father. The blind man crept off alone to beg for a few pieces of cash from the kind passers-by.

"One day he stumbled into a ditch. While he was trying to climb out of it, a firm hand lifted him up, and a voice spoke to him, 'Give me three hundred bags of rice for the temple, Old Man, and in time you shall have your eyes once again.'

"Sim marveled at these words. When he found that the speaker was a priest from the temple on the mountain near by, he believed the man's promise and hope filled his heart. But when he repeated it to his daughter, sadness swallowed his hope.

" '*Ai-go! Ai-go!*' he wailed. 'There is no way for beggars like us to obtain so much rice.'

"But in a dream that night the dead mother of Chung told the girl of a way by which she might get the rice to give her father his sight again. The next morning the good daughter disguised herself in the big hat and the long coarse gray gown of a person in mourning for the dead. She covered her nose and her mouth with the thin white-cloth shield a mourner always carries before his face. So hidden, she made her way to the courtyard of a certain rich merchant.

"This man owned many boats which carried cargoes of rice to faraway China, but of late the River Dragon had barred his way by throwing the water up in dangerous waves. The toll for safe passage which the Dragon demanded was a beautiful girl. The merchant had offered no less than three hundred bags of rice to that one who would offer herself for the sacrifice.

"The merchant was sorrowful when he heard Chung's sad story. 'So dutiful a daughter,' he said, 'does not deserve to die.' But there was no other way for her to get the rice, so the bargain was made.

"Chung's heart was glad when she watched the long line of horses, carrying the bags of rice to the priest's temple up in the hills. But her heart was sad when the priest told her it might take many years for her father to see again.

"The girl bowed before the tomb of her mother and prayed her to send heavenly spirits to care for the old man until he should be cured. She also gave the blind man over into the care of her good neighbors. Then she set forth to keep her part of the bargain she had made with the merchant.

"When she was dressed for her journey to the Dragon's watery realm, Chung shone brighter than the sun in the eastern heavens. Clad in a bride's gown of green, and with jewels and bright ribbons in her wedding headdress, she rode at the head of the merchant's procession of rice boats.

"Soon they came to the place in the river where the Dragon barred the way with the lashings of his great tail. To save this poor girl, the merchant offered to give many bags of his rice to the river spirit. All on the boats wept for their hearts were touched at her great love for her old blind father. They, too, made prayers, but the River Dragon would not be satisfied by any substitute for Chung.

"So the girl bowed to Heaven and jumped off the side of the boat. Straightway, my son, the angry waters grew as calm as those of our garden pool. The boats passed safely across them and went on their way to the Flowery Kingdom of China.

"Whether many fish drew her in a shell, or whether she was carried along by the dragon servants of the Sea King, Chung never knew. She found herself floating between waving undersea plants, amid bright-colored fish. She caught glimpses of pearls as big as your fist and of walls of black marble. Then she was led into the palace of the Sea King himself.

"The bewildered girl bowed before this Jade River Dragon, and said, 'Honorable sir, I am only the daughter of the blind beggar, Sim. I am not worthy to come before one so exalted as you.'

"But the Sea King replied, 'The light of the stars finds its way down to our undersea kingdom, and a message about you has come to us from Hananim, the Emperor of Heaven and Earth. You will be well rewarded for your goodness to your blind father.'

"Sea maidens dressed Chung in fine robes. They spread out before her soft sleeping mats, and they gave her rich food. In this life of comfort and ease the girl grew more beautiful than ever before.

"One day her attendants led Chung to a giant lotus blossom that lay on the river bottom. It was so large that they could hide her away within its fragrant heart. The

Sea King bade her farewell, and the girl felt herself rising up through the water. Soon, to her amazement, she saw the lotus flower was floating upon the river, close to the boat of her friend, the rice merchant.

" 'Never in Heaven or on earth was there such a lotus flower as this,' the boatmen said to the merchant. 'It must go to the King.' They were richly paid for it, and the King treasured none of his princely possessions so much as this rare, giant blossom. He went daily to see it in the special garden pool on which he set it to float.

"Only at night did Chung come out of her hiding place in the giant flower. Somehow its perfume served her as food, and the dew on its petals quenched her thirst.

"In the moonlight one evening the King came upon the girl as she walked on the bank of the crystal pool.

"Modestly she turned to hide herself from his sight, but her lotus-blossom shelter had vanished. The King was afraid at first she might be a spirit, but her beauty delighted him. The wise men who studied the heavens declared that on the day the lotus flower was brought to him by the boatmen, a bright new star had appeared overhead in the sky. With this good omen to reassure him, the King made Chung his wife."

"What became of the blind beggar, her father?" asked Ok Cha, who had come quietly into the room.

"That is the very best part of the tale, blessed girl," the Korean grandmother answered. "Now Chung was happy, as who would not be if she were a queen. But there were times when her heart also was sad. She thought often of her poor father, whose eyes were no doubt still closed to the world about him. One day her husband, the King, came upon her weeping as she sat in the garden.

"'*Ai-go*, great and excellent one,' Chung said to the King when he asked why she wept. 'It is a dream I have had about a blind man. His plight touches my heart. I should like to do something for all the blind in your kingdom. I should like to give them a fine feast.'

"One day, two days, and three days, the blind beggars of the land came to eat rice and *kimchee* in the King's courtyard. Peering at them through curtains, Queen Chung had hoped each one might prove to be her father. But the end of the feast came without Sim's appearing. The servants were just turning away a latecomer when the Queen recognized him through his tatters. She gave a loud cry. 'Abuji! Abuji! It is my dear father.' And she ordered the servants to be paddled for handling him so roughly.

"They dressed Sim, the blind beggar, in new clothing and brought him into the Queen's chamber.

"'What wonder is this?' said the blind man when he heard his dear daughter's voice. 'Do apricots bloom in the snow? Do horses have horns? Do the dead come to life? How can I be sure you are truly Chung unless I can see?' The old man rubbed his dim eyes, and suddenly, as the temple priest had foretold, his sight returned.

"When the King heard the tale, he heaped honors upon the father of his beloved Queen. He gave him a fine house. He appointed him to a high position at court. He even found him a wife to look after his food and his clothes in his old age.

"Then was Queen Chung happy all the day long. Then, indeed, was fulfilled the Sea King's promise of a heavenly reward to this dutiful daughter of the blind beggar, Sim."

THE MAN

WHO LIVED

A

THOUSAND

YEARS

THERE was great excitement in the Kim courts. The New Year, best of all holidays, was approaching. The big teakwood lanterns were getting their new flowered-paper panes. The beeswax candles were being counted. The needles of the women were flying to finish the New Year clothes for the family—white silk padded jackets, trousers, and skirts for the women and men, and bright green, red, and purple winter garments for the young children.

Yong Tu and Ok Cha and their cousins also were busy. The little girls were making bright paper flowers, and the boys were putting the finishing touches on their kites for the New Year contests. And as usual, Halmoni's room was the center of most of the family activity.

One afternoon when everyone sat there, bent over his work, Kim Dong Chin, Halmoni's second son, came seeking his mother.

"Here are the four pieces of the gate charm, Omoni," he said. "Shall I bind them up for you?"

"The thorn branches! The straw ox shoe! The foxtail grass! The salt bag! *Yé*, they are all here." The old woman nodded her head in satisfaction as she examined with critical eyes the curious collection before her. "*Yé*, bind them up!"

Yong Tu laid his kite down with great care and helped his uncle to tie the thorn wood, the ox shoe, and the foxtail grass inside the old salt bag. They made a neat packet about as long as an ironing club. Then the boy followed the man to the Outer Court, where the charm was firmly fastened above the bamboo gate.

"Why do we put such things over our gate, Halmoni?" Yong Tu asked his grandmother when he had returned to his kite making.

"Why else but to keep the bad spirits away, stupid boy? No charm is more powerful than this one. Each year a new gate charm must be made, lest the old one should be worn out by the wind and the weather and have perhaps lost its strength. I do not mean to be caught napping without such a charm, like old Tong Pang Suk. He had already lived for one thousand years; but if he'd held fast to his bundle of thorn wood and ox shoe, salt bag and foxtail, he'd no doubt be living still."

"A man who lived one thousand years, Halmoni?" Ok Cha questioned, her narrow black eyes shining with amazement.

"Some say Tong Pang Suk lived ten thousand years, precious ones, but my father declared that was far too long. One thousand years he lived surely. It probably happened because someone was careless in the Heavenly Emperor's Hall of Recording. There were kept the Books of Life in which all men's names are written down, so that the judges can determine the time for each one to be brought to the Jade Emperor's Heavenly Kingdom.

"Perhaps it happened that the pages for Tong Pang Suk were stuck together, or perhaps the judges turned them too fast before the book was put away behind the panels. But, whatever the reason, that old man's name was overlooked and no messenger was sent to take his spirit away from the earth.

"Even when Tong had lived out the full course of a man's life, no summons came. What could he do? He grew no older, for he was old as a man could be. He simply lived on and on, one hundred, two hundred, three hundred years.

"The friends of his childhood, long since departed to the Distant Shore, missed their old neighbor Tong. 'How is it?' they said to one another, and to the Jade Emperor as well. 'How is it that Tong Pang Suk remains so long on the earth?'

"One hundred, two hundred, three hundred years more it was before his pages in the Book of Life were found, and a messenger was finally sent to bring Tong Pang Suk up to Heaven. That messenger was a spirit, of course, but he took on the form of a man. Like Chung, the blind beggar's daughter, he disguised himself in the garb of a mourner. Hidden under his great hat, he wandered over the earth, looking for Tong.

"By this time Tong had become used to his great age. His days were calm, without wind and without cloud. And he spent most of them on the bank of a stream lost in the pleasures of fishing. The old man had no wish to die. His greatest fear was that the Heavenly Messenger might one day catch up with him. Each sixty years he took on a new name and he sought a new village so that he could not be traced. But always he fished.

"Somehow the Spirit Messenger heard of this old, old man who sat, always fishing, on a river bank. He thought perhaps this might be the one whom he sought, and he set a trap for him. Not far from where Tong fished, the Spirit Messenger threw many bags of charcoal into the river. Its black dust clouded the water so that it looked like ink paste.

" 'Why did you do that foolish trick?' Old Tong inquired when he found the source of the blackness that was spoiling his fishing.

" 'O, honorable grandfather, I'm just washing my charcoal. Soon it will be as white as the jacket you wear,' the Spirit replied.

" '*Ai! Ai!*' exclaimed Tong, shaking his head. 'I have dwelt in this land for nine hundred years, but never before have I met a man foolish enough to think he could wash black charcoal white.'

"The Spirit was happy now, for he knew he had found the man he was seeking. He followed Old Tong wherever he went, hoping for a chance to carry him off to the Other World. So close did he keep to the old man's heels that Tong Pang Suk guessed who he might be.

" 'You are brave, learned sir,' Tong said to his spirit companion one day. 'The country roads here are dangerous. Are you not afraid to travel so far upon them?'

" 'I fear not the country roads, nor any dangers upon them,' replied the Spirit who, in truth, was not nearly so quick-witted as Tong. 'There are but four things on this earth that I greatly fear, and wherever they are, there I am not.'

" 'What are the four things the Great Man fears?' Tong asked politely.

" 'A branch of a thorn tree, the shoe of an ox, foxtail grass, and a salt bag. Those four put together would bring me to my doom.

" 'And you, venerable father,' the Spirit asked in his turn, 'what do you fear the most?'

"Now Tong, for all he was so old, was crafty and wise. 'The things I fear most of all,' he said to the Spirit, 'are roast suckling pig and the beer called *mackalee.*'

"Marvels come to man more often than you may think, my children. And a marvel happened that day. Suddenly beside their path Old Tong saw foxtail grass growing beneath a thorn tree. By the side of the road near it he found a castoff straw ox shoe and an old empty salt bag.

"Gathering up the shoe and the bag, the old man quickly left the road and took refuge beneath the thorn tree. He plucked a thorn branch from over his head. He gathered some foxtail grass from under his feet. Thus quickly he completed the charm, and he tied all four parts of it into a bundle, just like the one on our gate.

"From a safe distance the unhappy Spirit begged the old man to come forth from under the thorn tree. He wept and he raged, but he dared not approach because of the charm.

"Then the Spirit remembered Old Tong's words about the things he feared most. He went off to the village and fetched a roast suckling pig and a jug of *mackalee* beer. These he flung at Old Tong, hoping to drive him out of his refuge.

"Instead, to his amazement, the Spirit saw the old man eating the roast pig with great gusto and drinking the *mackalee* beer with delight. He shook his head in bewilderment, and he gave up his idea of whisking Tong up to Heaven that day.

"But the Spirit Messenger was not yet beaten. He did not fly back to Heaven and give up his quest. For a hundred years more he waited and watched, hoping Tong would forget to carry with him the bundle he had made of the thorn wood and the foxtail grass, the ox shoe, and the salt bag.

"At last the Spirit Messenger's patience had its reward. One day the old man did forget his good charm as he set forth to fish, and the Spirit carried him off to the Heavenly Realm.

"Since then, all people who know the secret of Tong and his charm use this way of making sure of protection from evil spirits. It does not keep them from going to the Heavenly Kingdom when their time comes, but it drives many bad spirits away from their courts. Find me a house in all this street of ours without such a gate charm, and I'll show you a family with whom bad luck dwells."

A

FORTUNE

FROM

A FROG

Yong Tu and his cousins were getting ready to take part in the New Year kite flying contest.

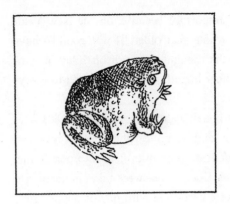

B RING a gift for our guest, Yong Tu," the Master of the Kim household called to his son, clapping his hands to summon him to his side. For the hundredth time in this first week of the New Year, the boy ran to the heap of guest presents laid out in his father's library. This visitor was an important guest, and at his father's suggestion Yong Tu brought forth a roll of fine silk.

What an exciting season the New Year was! Visitors constantly came and went through the Kims' bamboo gate. Sedan chairs, bringing Halmoni's guests, were escorted into the Inner Court. There, when the bearers had gone away, the women could safely crawl out from behind the chair curtains without fear of being seen by any strange men.

The Kim houses looked very fine with the new paper on their walls, on their floors, and in the panes of their latticed windows. The paper flowers the little girls had made brightened the rooms. The best embroidered screens were set out, and the finest wall poems were hung. Each member of the family had on his shining new silken clothes.

The children felt important because, on the New Year, each had become a whole year older. It was good to have two birthdays, Ok Cha thought, her own birthday in summer, and this New Year birthday which belonged to everyone.

"Bring cakes and honey water for our guests, Ok Cha," Halmoni said again and again during these days. The golden drink with delicate pine nuts floating upon it was a favorite in the Inner Court. The sweet cakes made of rice flour or bean flour were decorated with bits of popped rice, colored bright pink and green. There were little raven cakes, too, so called because of the old story of the raven which warned the King that a robber was hiding inside the Queen's zither case.

Ok Cha and the other children liked best of all the candy made of pine nuts and honey, this was the only sweetening Koreans knew in those long-ago times before sugar was brought from over the sea.

"Eat! Eat!" was the invitation on all sides at the New Year. Koreans always like food and a great deal of food, but especially at the New Year season everyone ate as much as his stomach could possibly hold. That foretold the plenty he would have throughout the year.

"Drink! Drink that your ears may be sharpened in the months to come!" people said. Even the small children then took a cup of the "good-hearing" wine.

There were guest presents in the Inner Court as well as in the reception room of the men. Halmoni looked with satisfied smiles at the huge piles of gifts, ready for the giving. There were hairpins of silver with their designs picked out with sky-blue kingfisher feathers and dotted with coral. There were boxes of shining black and red lacquer, bits of embroidery, and pieces of silk. There were gay ornaments for the headdress of a bride, as well as candies and cakes.

"Our gifts are worthy this year, Ok Cha," the Korean grandmother said to the little girl one afternoon early in the New Year season, while they sat waiting for the next visitor to appear.

"How many there are, Halmoni! Oh, I do think they are beautiful!"

"*Yé*, child, they are beautiful, and they are many. They remind me of the presents Lah and his wife received from the frog, but of course those were even richer."

"Is that a story, Halmoni? Tell me about the frog and his rich gifts," the little girl begged, sitting down carefully so as not to harm her new skirt.

"*Yé*, it's a story, Jade Child. It's a story fit for the New Year, for it tells of good fortune. The good fortune came to a poor couple named Lah, who lived in a hut on the Diamond Mountains. Both the man and his wife were unhappy because under their grass roof there was no son to pray to their spirits when they should have gone beyond the Earthly Gates. And they were too poor to adopt a boy to bring up as their son, who might perform this service for them.

"Their fields on the mountain sides gave this couple only enough rice to keep them alive. The cabbage, turnips, and peppers they could raise in their rocky garden made only enough *kimchee* for their own eating bowls. They had hens which laid a few eggs, and they found honey in the nests of the wild bees in the rocks. So they did not starve.

"For buying their clothes and their salt they depended on the fish which Lah caught in the nearby mountain lake and which he sold in the village in the valley below. So you can guess he was distressed when, one morning, he saw that his lake had dried up and the fish had all disappeared. On the bank sat a giant frog, as big as a man. It was just finishing drinking up the lake water.

" 'Wicked frog,' poor Lah scolded. 'What demon possessed you to drink up my lake and to devour my fish? Have I not enough trouble without such a disaster?'

"But the frog only bowed politely and replied in a soft voice, 'Honorable sir, I, too, regret the disappearance of the lake, for that was my home. Now I have no shelter. Pray give me refuge under your roof.'

"At first, Lah refused, as he had good reason for doing. But the gentle words of the frog softened his heart. His wife also objected when her husband led the giant frog into their hut. But it was lonely there on the mountain side, and the woman was interested in the good tales the frog told. She brought in leaves to serve as his bed, and she thoughtfully fetched water to make it comfortably damp to suit a frog's taste.

"Early the next morning, Lah and his wife were wakened at dawn by the sound of loud croaking. The din was as great as that of soothsayers trying to drive evil spirits from the stomach of a sick man. Hurrying out on their veranda, they saw the giant frog lifting his croaking voice to the heavens. But their eyes soon turned away from the reddening eastern sky to the shining treasures they saw in their courtyard.

"Our New Year gifts could not compare with those the

frog had provided for his good hosts. There were strings upon strings of copper cash, and valuable silver coins, too. There were fat bags of rice, great jars of *kimchee*, packets of seaweed, and good salt fish. Rolls of cotton and silk cloth; hats, padded stockings, and new quilted shoes; fans, pipes, and rich ornaments of silver and gold! *Ai*, who can say what there was not in the fortune that frog brought to Lah and his wife?

"In the fine sedan chair the frog gave her, Lah's wife began to take journeys down into the inner courts of the valley houses. She made friends with the women there, and from them she learned more and more about the people of that neighborhood.

" 'Tell me about Yun Ok,' the frog always asked when the woman returned. Yun Ok, or Jade Lotus, was the youngest daughter of the richest *yangban* in all that northern province. She was, so the gossip of the inner courts had it, by far the most beautiful girl in the land. Her skin was like a pale cloud. Her eyes and her hair were as black as a raven's wing. Her form was as graceful as bamboo bent by the spring breeze.

" 'It is Yun Ok I must marry, Omoni,' the frog said to Lah's wife, whom he now was permitted to think of as his mother. 'Go, honorable Lah, go now and ask for Yun Ok for my bride.'

" 'I shall surely be paddled.' Lah trembled at the thought of asking the great *yangban's* daughter to marry a frog. But the golden words of the frog persuaded him. He went, clad in such fine clothes that the servants of the *yangban* swiftly admitted him to his Hall of Guests.

"Now the two older daughters of this family had married worthless young men, and the proud father of Yun Ok was determined his youngest daughter should have a better husband.

" 'Is this suitor rich?' he demanded of Lah.

" 'Yes, great sir, he is rich.'

" 'What kind of jade button does he wear in his hat?' he inquired, which is the same as to ask what government office he holds.

" 'Well,' said Lah, 'that I cannot exactly say.'

" 'Is he handsome? What is his name?' All these were the questions the father of a daughter always asks of a go-between who comes to arrange a marriage.

" 'You could not call him handsome, I think,' the poor man replied. 'And his name? He is called Frog, for a frog he is. But he is a frog as large as a man, and golden words come from his mouth.'

" 'A frog! This is an insult! Bring out the paddles,' the angry *yangban* shouted. Unlucky Lah was seized and laid down on the ground, ready for a severe paddling. The servants raised the dreaded clubs with their hard, flattened ends. They were about to give Lah a terrible beating when dark clouds covered the sun. Lightning flashed. Such terrible thunder was heard that the men dropped their paddles in terror. Only when the *yangban* gave orders to untie Lah did the sun fill the heavens and earth with bright light again.

" 'This is surely a sign from the Jade Emperor of Heaven,' the *yangban* said sadly, and he consented to the marriage of his daughter, Yun Ok, to the frog.

"That must have been a curious sight, a giant frog sitting on the white horse of a bridegroom. Of course the bride could not see it, for according to custom her eyes were sealed shut with wax. It was not until the wedding feast had been eaten that Yun Ok found out she had married a giant frog.

" 'Do not weep, Yun Ok,' her strange bridegroom tried to comfort her. 'Wait just a little!' And when they were alone in the bridal chamber, he gave her a sharp knife to slit his frog's skin up the back. When he wriggled out of the skin, the frog stood before her, a fine and handsome young man. Clad in a cloak of silk and wearing a button of finest jade in his topknot, he was a *yangban* of the *yangbans*. And he explained the strange happening thus:

" 'I am the son of the King of the Stars. My father, being displeased with some of my actions, decided to punish me. He sent me down to the earth in the form of a frog, and he commanded me to perform three unheard-of tasks. First, I was to eat all the fish in a lake and to drink its waters dry. Second, I must persuade a human couple to adopt me, a frog, as their son. Third, I must marry the loveliest lady in all the land. Only then could I return to his starry kingdom. Those three tasks have been done. But the hour of my return is not yet. When I go, Yun Ok, I will take you to dwell with me in the sky.'

"The delighted bride sewed her handsome husband back into his frog's skin, and he went off on the journey a bridegroom always takes after the wedding, lest it should be thought he liked his new wife too well. While he was gone, Yun Ok only smiled when her sisters and their foolish husbands made fun of her frog.

"Her *yangban* father, although he had given consent, was not pleased with the marriage. His sixty-first birthday was near, and as everyone knows, that is the most important occasion in any man's life. All members of his family were invited to a great feast—all, that is, except his frog son-in-law. And to provide the food for the feast, his other two sons-in-law were sent out to hunt game and to bring fish from the rivers and lakes.

"When the frog heard of the feast, he called to him the king of the tiger clan. 'Take all the wild beasts, both little and big, into your cave, Mountain Uncle!' he said. 'Let there be none for those hunters.' He likewise summoned the king of the fishes and gave him the command to hide all the finny creatures on the bottoms of the rivers and lakes. So there was no game for the hunters, no fish for the fishermen, and no food at all for the birthday feast.

"The *yangban* was dismayed. But as he wrung his hands over his plight, there came into his gates a procession such as had never been seen in his courts. Horses bearing wild boars and tender young deer; fish of all kinds; wild ducks and more game than the guests could possibly eat.

"At the head of the procession was a chair covered with tiger skins and borne by sixteen men. In it rode a splendid young man. You can guess the *yangban* was surprised when he learned that this shining Prince was in truth his youngest daughter's despised husband, who had worn the frog's skin.

"The *yangban* bowed before the Star Prince, although that is not the custom between a man and his son-in-law. He begged forgiveness for his neglect, and he offered the frog-husband the seat of honor at the feast.

"But the Star Prince only bade his bride make ready for their long journey, and a great cloud from Heaven snatched them up to the sky. That night the wise men who study the heavens found two new stars shining brightly just over-head. What else could they be but the fair Yun Ok and her frog, the son of the Star King?

"The fortune brought to Lah by the frog lasted throughout his whole life. His riches grew ever greater and greater, and he wore the jade button in his official hat. Through all the twelve months it was New Year in his courts."

THE

GREAT

FIFTEENTH

DAY

I WASHED my face nine times, Yong Tu, and I cleaned my teeth with salt nine times, too," Ok Cha said to her brother on the morning of the Fifteenth Day of the First Month.

"I combed my hair nine times, and I shall eat nine kinds of nuts today," the Korean boy replied.

It was the Great Fifteenth Day, the day which ended the New Year holiday season, and it was the last chance to make sure of the New Year good luck. Each child raced with the others to see how many "lucky nines" he could collect during the day.

The women also believed the number nine would bring them good luck. They gladly prepared the nine meals for the family; they swept the floors nine times; and nine times they stuffed fuel into the stove. The Master of the House himself bowed nine times before the tablets in the Ancestors' House.

This dignified father of Ok Cha and Yong Tu was careful to omit none of the usual doings of this day. Under his watchful eyes his younger brothers and the boys made the three straw figures which should represent each of the three men of the household. To hide amid the straw, he gave them pieces of cash, Korean copper coins with big holes cut in their centers. He decided which old coats should be put upon the straw manikins. Together, all the men and boys of the household went to the gate to see the straw men tossed out into the street.

"You should have seen the street boys fall on our straw men, Halmoni," Yong Tu reported to his grandmother. "They pulled off the old garments, and they tore at the straw to get the cash out."

"That is well, my grandson." The old woman nodded her head in great satisfaction. "The more they kick the straw figures, the luckier our men will be. The bad spirits will be well fooled. They will think those are truly your father and uncles. The good spirits will read the paper prayers you tucked inside them. They will then help keep away ill luck from our house."

Yong Tu himself wrote the prayers on the strips of paper hidden inside the straw figures. With careful brush strokes he had written this sentence on each, "For the coming twelve months, from sickness and bad luck protect me." The boy had kept watch through the bamboo gate until he could be sure that the straw figures were well kicked apart.

"All the bad luck of the past year has gone with those straw men," the Korean grandmother told the children. "Your fathers can now make a fresh start. They have cast out their old, unlucky selves. Today they are new men, beginning a new year."

Sometimes Ok Cha and Yong Tu thought the Great Fifteenth Day was even better than the New Year itself.

This two-weeks New Year holiday, with its visitors and its gifts, its delicious food and its firecrackers to drive off the spirits, were filled with pleasures. The seesaw was in constant motion. The girls, standing upright upon it, were tossed higher and higher into the air. Even Mai Hee, or Plum Child, Halmoni's oldest granddaughter, enjoyed this sport.

No Korean girl of those times would have wished to seesaw sitting down. That was not the custom. Also, it would not have been nearly so breath-taking as to be bounced high in the air, and then to come down neatly again on one's two feet. For making safe landings, little girls like Ok Cha clung to a balance rope hung from over their heads.

"My father used to say," Halmoni explained, "the reason seesaws were invented was because girls grew tired of being shut up inside the Inner Court. When they bounced high into the air, they could look out over the walls into the street beyond."

On this Great Fifteenth Day the sky above the Kim courts was dotted with kites. Those that were lowest showed their red, green, and purple colorings. Those higher up were like a flock of dark birds, flying across the blue sky.

Yong Tu and his cousins had finished the kites they were making for the contest to be held on this day. With strong silken thread they had carefully tied two splints of bamboo across each other to form a giant letter *X*. They had run other silk threads from end to end on these rods, to form the outside frame of the kite. Then they had covered the frame well with fine Korean paper, made from the bark of the mulberry tree. They took care to leave the center crossing uncovered, cutting out a small disc of the paper, so that the silken kite string could be tied to the bamboo splints. The reels for the kite strings were as carefully made as were the kites themselves.

Halmoni had provided bits of old pottery which the boys pounded into tiny sharp bits for coating their kite strings. Running the strings first through sticky glue, then through the powdered pottery, they gave them a good cutting edge. For in kite fighting it was the string that could cut in two any other string crossing it, which won the day. Yong Tu was proud because he managed to keep his kite longest up in the air. Of all the kitefliers of his age, he thus became the champion.

"The very first of such 'flying ones' was made hundreds and hundreds of years ago," Halmoni said to Ok Cha and the other girls, as they stood in the Inner Court and watched Yong Tu's kite make its triumphant flight from the street beyond the bamboo gate. "It was during one of the many times when the 'dwarf men of Japan' came here to try to conquer our country. The battles were not going well for the soldiers of our Little Kingdom. One night a star shot across the sky like an arrow, over their heads. An arrow star, as everyone knows, is a sign of bad luck. All were discouraged. They were sure they would lose in the next day's fighting. The general it was who thought of a

The seesaw was in constant motion during the New Year holidays. The girls standing upright upon it were tossed higher and higher into the air.

way to lift up their spirits. He made a large kite, and he tied a small lantern fast to its frame. Then he sent it flying high in the sky.

"When the soldiers saw the lantern's light, they shouted, 'Here's a good sign! A new star hangs in the sky. A sure omen of victory!' And the next day they fought with renewed courage and might, and the enemy was driven away."

Halmoni liked to explain about the different doings of the Great Fifteenth Day to the children.

"Tonight, out on the hills, the farmers will gather to watch the full moon rise, my blessed ones. By its color on this night they will know whether their crops will be good in the coming season. If the moon is too pale, that means there will be too much rain. If it is too red, there will not be nearly enough, and the rice plants will dry up. But if it is a rich yellow, the color of a golden chrysanthemum, there will be just enough rain and more than enough rice to keep the spirits of hunger away from their gates.

"And the farmers will dig up their bamboo and their beans to find out in just which months the good rains will come," the old Korean grandmother continued. She described how each farmer had split a section of young bamboo and laid twelve little beans side by side within it. He then had tied the halves of the bamboo together again and covered it lightly with earth, where it could be moistened by rain and by dew.

"Each of those beans stands for one of the twelve months," Halmoni said. "When the farmer digs it up tonight and opens the bamboo case, he will examine each little bean. The ones that are dampest will be the months in which the most rain will come."

In the city, too, there were special doings on the night of the Great Fifteenth Day. The men and boys "walked the bridges," crossing once for every year of their age. They carried with them picnic baskets filled with good things so that they might eat and drink with friends whom they met upon the bridges.

Of all the events of the day for Yong Tu, most exciting was the great stone fight outside the city on the bare wintry fields.

"You should have seen that fight this afternoon, Halmoni," the boy said to his grandmother when they were eating their evening rice. "*Ai*, it was like a battle, and many people were hurt. The teams lined up facing each other. The men had pads on their shoulders and special hats to protect their heads. You should have heard them shout when those stones began to fly. You should have seen how clever they were at dodging them, too. One stone—but only a little one, Halmoni—flew so close to my father's head that it knocked his hat off. *Hé*, I was almost afraid. But the hat was not hurt," the boy hastened to add. "And my father did not mind. He was shouting as loudly as the rest of the crowd."

"Too many heads are broken in the stone fights," the old woman declared. "It is not as if it were a true battle. It has no such good purpose as had the very first stone fight."

"Tell me about the very first stone fight, Halmoni," the boy begged. "Was it long ago?"

"Very, very long ago, Dragon Head," the old grandmother said, nodding her head. "How long ago nobody seems to know. Perhaps it was when the tall horsemen galloped over our land from that northern place called Mongolia. Perhaps it was their chieftain, Genghis Khan himself, who led those fierce horsemen to conquer us. Or, it may have been later when the Chinese came across our neighbor-land, Manchuria, in quest of our treasures.

"But whenever it was, it was in the midst of a war. The battle which was the key to the victory was being fought. A brave Korean general had lined his men up above a narrow pass in the mountains. His soldiers were as courageous and strong as any tiger, but their gunpowder gave out. A tiger could not fight without teeth or claws. How could our soldiers fight without any gunpowder?

"That is the question the general asked himself when he lay down to sleep on this night. His heart was indeed heavy, and his rest was disturbed. But in his dreams, a good Spirit came to him and said, 'Be not dismayed! Under a tree, not far away, you will find a heap of stones. Throw these down on your enemy, and you will drive him away.'

"With his dream fresh in his mind the general called his men to the tree and showed them the pile of stones. Like rain, the brave soldiers sent the sharp rocks flying down on the heads of their advancing foe. More and more stones were hurled until all the foe had been killed.

"When the strange battle was reported to the Emperor, he took delight in seeing it enacted before him again in his palace courtyard. Each year thereafter, when the rice fields were bare and there was time for such sport, stone fights were held for his amusement.

"To meet future attacks from enemies from the north, that Emperor had many other piles of stones laid up beside the roads. The story of the good Spirit in the general's dream spread over the land. Travelers passing the stone piles began to throw pebbles upon them, with a prayer that the Spirit would protect them as it once had protected the general. Your father, Yong Tu, never fails to take this precaution when he travels out into the country to inspect our rice fields."

A KOREAN

CINDERELLA

THUMPITY-THUMP! Thumpity-thump!
The song of the ironing sticks sounded throughout
the Inner Court. On the narrow veranda outside her
apartment, the mother of Ok Cha and Yong Tu and one of
their aunts sat facing each other. Their white-stockinged
feet were tucked comfortably under their full white skirts.
Their hands flew deftly up and down, their ironing sticks
pounding the strips of fine white grass linen folded upon
the low oblong ironing stone between them.

Not far away two maidservants also were ironing. They
were pounding smooth the red, green, and blue garments
of the boys and girls of the household.

"The maids can be trusted to launder the clothing of the
women and children," her mother said to Ok Cha who stood
near by watching her, "but it is better that I myself iron
the outer coat of the Master of this House. It would not be
fitting that he should go forth from our gate with wrinkles
in his garments."

Thumpity-thump! Thumpity-thump! On and on sang the ironing clubs, two in each pair of hands.

"We are never done ironing here, Halmoni," Ok Cha said to her grandmother, who had come to see that the women were doing their work well. "Why do grown-up people always wear white? It grows dirty so quickly."

"Why should it be, save that it is the custom?" the old woman replied. "Some say that in earlier days men and women, like children, wore bright-colored garments. Then it so happened that the Queen died, and all laid aside their reds, blues, and greens and put on the white of sadness. No sooner was their time of mourning for the Queen over than the King died. Then all must put on their white mourning garments again. There was one death after another in that royal family, and the people of our nation became so used to their white clothes that they never changed back to bright colors again.

"But I never believed that tale, blessed girl. White is the color we love best of all. It stands for goodness and wisdom. Our people have preferred it above all other colors for thousands of years. That is why we like to wear white."

The women of the Inner Court of the Kim family were seldom idle. Each garment had to be ripped apart before it was laundered. And it had to be sewed up again when it had been ironed. It was far easier, they thought, to give the proper shine to flat pieces of cloth than to coats, jackets, skirts, and full pantaloons.

"How would you like to do all our family ironing, Little Ok Cha?" the Korean grandmother asked, as she walked with the child around the corner of the women's houses and into the Garden of Green Gems.

"I could never do that, Halmoni. Nobody could." Ok Cha looked horrified at the very thought.

"But that is what the poor girl, Nan Yang, or Orchid Blossom, had to do for her cruel stepmother and her selfish stepsisters. The story was told to me by my grandmother, and I have no doubt she spoke truly. But then, of course, Nan Yang was bigger than you. She had seen fifteen New Years, and she was old enough to be married."

"Tell me the story about Nan Yang, Halmoni. Let's sit down under the pear tree, here in the shade."

All about the old woman and the little girl were the flowers of early summer. The soft air was filled with the perfume of the garden, and it was pleasantly cool under the pear tree.

"Nan Yang was the daughter of a village official, my precious," Halmoni began. "Her own mother had died, and her father had married again, a shrew of a woman with two vain, selfish daughters.

"*Ai-go*, those newcomers had no love nor pity for that poor motherless Nan Yang. They made her work from the first light of the dawn to the coming of dark, and even far, far into the night. She must clean the rice, and she must fetch the water. She must bring the fuel for the hungry mouth of the stove, and she must sweep clean the court-yard, all by herself.

"Instead of using her own name, Nan Yang, or Orchid Blossom, they nicknamed her 'Dirty Pig.' As everyone knows, that is even worse than to be called a dog. Oh, they found many ways to make the girl weep.

"When her other work was at last done, they gave her the ironing sticks. To the sound of her pounding, these three selfish creatures fell asleep night after night. Nan Yang's father could do nothing, for he feared the sharp tongue of his new wife, as much as did the poor girl.

"Now in their country village one day, there was to be a fine fair. All the people were going—to hear the bright music, to see the comic acrobats, and to listen to the good tales of the traveling storyteller. There would be candy and cakes and other strange foods to buy.

" 'You may go to the fair, Dirty Pig,' the unkind stepmother said to Nan Yang, 'but only when you have husked this sack of rice, and only when you have filled this cracked jar with fresh water.'

"Nan Yang's father, clad in his new hat and his best long white coat, looked very sad. But he dared not oppose his shrewish wife. Poor Nan Yang wept as she watched them all depart for the fair, and she envied her stepsisters in their pretty new dresses of bright pink and green.

"With a sigh the sad girl began the tasks her stepmother had set her. But she had scarcely poured the sack of unhusked rice out on the ground when there was an odd swishing noise and a deafening twittering. These strange sounds came from the wings and the throats of ten thousand little birds, which lighted upon the great pile of rice. With their tiny sharp beaks the birds pecked off the husks. Almost before Nan Yang could dry her tears, the rice grains were white and clean. She had only to put them back into the sack again.

"Taking hope, the girl turned next to the broken water jar. But when she saw its great crack, she began to weep. 'However much water I pour into that jar, it will never be full,' she said aloud. But when she came back from the well with her first bucket, she found the crack mended with firm, hardened clay. No doubt it was a good *tokgabi* from the kitchen rafters who had taken pity upon her, like the ten thousand birds. No doubt it was that *tokgabi*, too, who bewitched this first bucket so that somehow there poured from it enough water to fill the great jar to the brim.

"Now Nan Yang could go to the fair to hear the music, to see the acrobats, and to listen to the storytellers' good tales. You can imagine, my pigeon, how surprised and displeased her stepmother and her stepsisters were to see her there so happy and enjoying herself.

"The next feast in that village was a picnic on the hillsides to view the summer scenery.

" 'You may go to the picnic, Dirty Pig,' her unkind stepmother said to Nan Yang, 'but only when you have dug out all the weeds in our rice field.' The cruel woman nodded her head, satisfied that the girl could never finish that task in time. And she had good reason to think this, for the rice field was large and the weeds were many.

"Nan Yang took up her hoe but when she struck its point into the very first clump of weeds, a huge black ox appeared close to her side. With mighty bites the animal dug all the weeds out of that field. In a dozen mouthfuls every weed had disappeared down its great throat.

" 'Come with me, Orchid Blossom,' the huge black ox commanded. And it led the girl off to the hillside and into the woods.

"When Nan Yang came at last to the picnic, her basket was filled with the ripest, the rarest, and the most delicious of fruits. All tne picnickers marveled at its excellent flavor. They made much of Nan Yang, to her stepsisters' dismay.

"At home that evening her stepmother demanded that Nan Yang tell them how she had managed to rid the rice field of weeds and where she found the fruit.

" 'We shall stay at home next time ourselves,' the selfish stepsisters declared when she told them the story. 'Nan Yang shall go ahead to the picnic before the black ox comes again.' "

"Did the black ox come to the selfish stepsisters, Halmoni?" Ok Cha asked when her grandmother paused to take breath.

"*Yé*, the ox came, Jade Child," the Korean woman replied. "And it led the selfish stepsisters also off into the woods. But it was not as it had been with the dutiful Nan Yang. To follow the black ox, the two selfish sisters had to crawl through tangled thickets. The twigs pulled out their hair, and the thorns tore their fine clothing. Their sullen faces were scratched. There was blood on their soft, idle hands. They made a sorry sight when they arrived at the picnic place. And there was no fruit at all in their battered baskets."

THE

RABBIT

THAT RODE

ON A

TORTOISE

TENDER green leaves cloaked the willow tree in the Garden of Green Gems beyond the Inner Court. Bright blossoms, like the pink-and-white clouds of the sunset, covered the fruit trees there. The waters of the little brook that fed the lotus pond was "clear as a teardrop," so Halmoni put it. On the damp garden path the earthworms had come forth to take their first looks at the Spring. All day the girls played blindman's buff and the boys spun their tops in the garden.

Out beyond the city the hillsides were carpeted with red, white, and purple azaleas. On bright afternoons little processions of picnickers wound their way out to them to view the mountains and valleys in their Spring beauty. Yong Tu had already brought back many azalea petals for the women to dry and use in making sweet, spicy cakes.

"*Ai*, this is the happy season," Halmoni said to the children one morning. The old woman was sitting on the steps of her little veranda, breathing in the soft scented air of late Spring.

"And this is a happy day, Halmoni. It's the Eighth Day of the Fourth Month. You know what day that is?" Ok Cha looked eagerly into her grandmother's calm face. The old woman seemed thoughtful. There was a twinkle in her dark eyes, but she also tried to look puzzled.

"What day is this?" she asked. "Oh yes, it's the birthday of the Wise Teacher, the Great Buddha." She smiled at the little girl, for she knew well that this old meaning of the day was not what Ok Cha had in mind. She enjoyed gently teasing her beloved small granddaughter.

"No, Halmoni, no. It's the Day of the Toys. What toys have you bought for our holiday this year?" The Korean girl's black eyes danced with delight at the thought of the pleasures of this holiday that was particularly for the children like her.

"Call Yong Tu and the others and you shall see, curious one," the grandmother replied. She rose from the steps and went into her room.

The children came running. In their red, green, and blue jackets, pantaloons, and full skirts, they looked even gayer than the bright blossoms in the stone pots beside the veranda steps.

Out of the drawers of a small brassbound chest Halmoni took one toy after another. She set them down in the center of the circle made by the children, squatting down on the floor.

"For me, the tiger with the Mountain God on his back." Yong Tu made his choice first because he was the oldest.

The girls were playing blindman's buff in the Garden of Green Gems.

One of his boy cousins reached for a little clay whistle made in the shape of a dove. The hollow gray bird had a hole in its back and a mouthpiece in its tail, so that when its new owner blew it, there was the sound of a dove's call, "Coo-roo! Coo-roo!"

Even fifteen-year-old Mai Hee was not above taking part in this giving of the toys. She chose a clay horse with a gaily dressed singing girl, a *gesang*, sitting upon it. The *gesang* held a bright-colored umbrella over her head. Only such singing girls and country girls who worked in the rice fields could go about freely. Girls such as Mai Hee always traveled shut up in a sedan chair. Perhaps Mai Hee secretly envied these less fortunate girls their greater freedom.

"I'd like the rabbit that rides on the tortoise." Ok Cha chose the same little toy every year. "And I'd like Halmoni to tell us the story about him."

"A rabbit is a clever animal, blessed girl," the old grandmother began, taking the little toy up in her hands. "He was far more clever than the tortoise he rode upon, who thought to get the best of him.

"It was on the seashore one day that this rabbit saw a strange tortoise crawling towards him. Now all rabbits are curious, as you well know. And, being so curious, this one stopped hopping and wiggled its nose. It waited to see what the strange tortoise would do.

"'Have you eaten your honorable food, sir?' the tortoise greeted the rabbit, just as politely as if he had been a man.

"'*Yé*, I have eaten. Have you been in peace, good sir?' the rabbit replied with a bow. 'What brings the Great Man here?'

" 'I came to explore these green hillsides,' the tortoise replied. 'I have heard that the view they give of the sea is very fine. I, too, wish to admire it.'

" 'Does it please your honorable eyes?' the rabbit asked.

" 'I find it very dull,' was the impolite answer. 'It cannot compare with the views of the sea from under the water. Here on the land there are no waving plants of clear green, like the finest jade, such as there are in the undersea gardens. Here are no hills of coral, no valleys nor plains brightened by royal processions of fishes with rainbow scales. You should see for yourself the many beauties and treasures of the Dragon King's watery realm.'

" 'I should like to witness such wonders,' said the rabbit, whose curiosity once again had got the better of his good judgment. 'But I cannot swim. How should I travel there?'

" 'You could swim there on my back, honorable rabbit,' the tortoise said persuasively. 'I go so slowly that you would not fall off, and I could teach you to breathe under the water as well as upon the land.'

"Now that tortoise, my grandchildren, spoke with honey upon his lips, but he had a knife in his heart. He meant no good to that rabbit, as you shall hear.

"You should know that the best-beloved daughter of the Dragon King had been ill for many a day. No one had been able to cure her. Not the great whale, nor yet the little shrimp. Though the king had offered a rich reward, none had succeeded in finding a way to drive the evil spirts out of her body.

"Then the tortoise had come forward, and said, 'I have heard, exalted sir, that the best cure for any ailment is the liver of a young rabbit. I know where I can find such a one. I think I can bring him here so that his liver may work the cure for your daughter.'

"The Dragon King had then renewed his hope of saving his daughter. He had sent the tortoise off to the seashore to bring back the rabbit. Now the tortoise is not very clever. Everyone knows that. Or why should he creep about dragging his tail in the dirt? But he was clever enough not to let the rabbit know why he was so anxious to ferry him down to the undersea palace of that Dragon King.

"As the story tells it, the rabbit did indeed become used to breathing under the water. He did indeed see shining wonders such as the tortoise had promised. His round eyes grew rounder at the sight of the gems and the treasures in the Dragon King's palace. He enjoyed himself greatly. But then he overheard one of the fish guards at the entrance to the Dragon King's court, say to another, 'Now that this rabbit has come, the Dragon King's daughter will surely recover. Today they will cut his liver out of his body. She will eat up his liver and she will be cured.'

"The dismayed rabbit gathered his wits quickly together. When they came to take out his liver, he showed no sign of fear.

" 'Why did the tortoise not tell me it was my liver you wanted?' he said to the Dragon King, bowing politely. 'Did he not know that when Hananim made us rabbits, he gave us the power to take our livers out of our bodies? When I eat too much and my liver grows hot, I remove it and cool it in the blue ocean waves. When I met the tortoise, I had just put my liver out on the beach to dry in the sun. You might have had it without so much bother, for I do not really need it myself. But now we shall have to go all the way back to get it.'

"The Dragon King and the tortoise believed the words of the rabbit. With his tail dragging even lower in shame the tortoise let the rabbit mount again upon his back. And he ferried him across the ten thousand flashing blue waves to the safe, sunny beach.

" 'Where does your liver lie, honorable rabbit?' asked the tortoise, who was eager to repair his mistake.

" '*Ai*, it's safe inside my body. And now I am safe, too!' the rabbit cried gaily, bounding away across the sand like a young deer.

"If rabbits can laugh, my children, I am sure that rabbit laughed until his long ears shook like a rooster's tail in a high wind."

LETTERS

FROM

HEAVEN

THE needle in Halmoni's fingers flew back and forth through the pale green silk of the screen panel she was embroidering. As she stitched in the golden beak of a rose-colored stork, her dark head moved in time to the singsong voice of Yong Tu.

The boy was sitting crosslegged on the floor. Half speaking, half chanting, he was repeating aloud a wise saying of the ancient Chinese teacher, Confucius. "Obedience to one's parents is the mother of one hundred virtues," he said again and again, trying to learn the proverb by heart.

The *Thousand Character Book* Yong Tu held in his lap had three different columns, running up and down its soft paper pages. There was first the column of characters, or word pictures, of Chinese writing. Then there was a middle column that told the boy how to pronounce them. The third column gave their meaning in *unmun*, which means words formed by the letters of the Korean alphabet.

"The Wise Confucius wrote that book in one single night," Halmoni told her grandson. "So great was the task that when morning came, his hair and his beard were turned white as the snow."

"The Chinese word pictures are hard to remember, there are so many, Halmoni," the boy complained. And he yawned a great yawn. "Now if this book were only written in *unmun*, I could read it straight through. Alphabet writing is so much easier than writing with word pictures."

"The young schoolman has wisdom," his grandmother replied smiling. *"Unmun* is indeed easier, but *unmun* does not bring true learning. The scholar whom the Dragon carries to the Highest Heaven must be the master of the learning of the ancient sages of China. Only such a one becomes the Great Man who faces a king without trembling. Only he dresses in fine silk, and only he wears the court seal at his belt. No young scholar should be frightened away from such rewards by a few difficult tasks.

"Everyone knows, Yong Tu, that our Korean 'low writing' is easy to learn. Ok Cha already has by heart the twenty-five letters of its alphabet, and she is but a girl who does not truly need to learn anything save the ways of the Inner Court." The Korean grandmother paused to pat the shoulder of her granddaughter and to retie the red bow on her long braid of black hair. Ok Cha was also learning a lesson that morning, a lesson in embroidery. She was stitching a bright red flower on a scrap of the green silk left from Halmoni's screen.

"Not even the King who invented our alphabet ever compared it with the jade writings from China," the Korean grandmother began again. "Not even when he told the people its letters came directly from Heaven."

"How could letters come from Heaven, Halmoni?" Yong

Tu asked. The boy hoped to prolong this pleasant pause in his morning study.

"*Hé,* blessed boy, who can say how messages come down to us from Heaven? Sometimes it is in a dream while one is asleep. Sometimes it is in a thought when one is awake. And sometimes it comes in the form of a sign or a miracle. For most people a miracle is always the best, and a miracle is what the good, wise King desired when he called on the earthworms to help him."

Ok Cha, too, put down her work when she heard these strange words spoken by her grandmother.

"It was thus it happened, they say, though it was so long ago that it is recorded only in this ancient story. A good King gave the precious gift of reading to our people through this *unmun* alphabet. He knew well that learning is the greatest treasure of man. He knew also that few of his subjects could master the thousands upon thousands of word pictures in the books that came to us from China.

"The King searched and searched for a simpler way of writing and reading. And because of a dream, or perhaps because he was so wise, that King reasoned thus: 'Words are made up of sounds, and sounds could be given symbols, or letters, that would stand for them. To learn, say, twenty-five letters would not be too difficult for any man, or even for any woman. By putting these letters together, all the words we need could be made.' And with his brush and his inkstone he carefully set down on paper the form of each one of the twenty-five letters of our alphabet.

"In those times, my children, as now, our people honored the customs of their ancestors. It would have been hard indeed for that good man, for all he was the King, to persuade them to adopt this new way of writing. 'They must have a sign from Heaven,' he decided. And doubtless here again it was a message from the Jade Emperor, up in the sky, that showed him the way.

"The King dipped his writing brush into a pot of honey. With its sticky sweetness he brushed each letter on the face of a tender green leaf. These leaves he spread out on the damp garden path where the earthworms could find them.

"His clever plan worked. The worms followed the sweet honey trails, eating their way along the face of the leaves. In this way they traced clearly the outlines of the twenty-five letters upon them.

" 'Here is a miracle,' the King called to his courtiers in the garden next day. 'Here clearly are messages sent us from Heaven, written on leaves.'

"Pretending he knew nothing of their hidden secret, he offered a reward to that scholar who should uncover their meaning. He took a young *paksa* into his confidence, and he gave him the task of explaining to the people the use that could be made of these 'letters from Heaven.'

"In this way our *unmun* alphabet was invented and spread over the land. In this way all people could learn to read if they would. Some tell other tales of its invention, but this is the one my grandmother believed."

"It was really just a trick, Halmoni, saying those letters came to us from Heaven," Ok Cha said knowingly.

"Who can say, precious Jade Child? But if it was a trick, it was a good trick. It gave books to people who never could have hoped to read otherwise. And it brought shining light into the darkness of women and girls who dwelt in the inner courts."

In Korea, in these days when Yong Tu and Ok Cha were children, learning was indeed prized above everything else. *Sobang*, which means "schoolman" was the polite common title. It was used just as *Mister* is in Western lands. Old Pak might be only a dark, unlearned gatekeeper, but he was pleased when a familiar peddler, entering the bamboo gate with his spices or silks, bowed to him, saying, "Peace, Sobang Pak, have you eaten your honorable meal?"

THE

MOURNER

WHO SANG

AND

THE NUN

WHO

DANCED

"How shall I ever become a *paksa*, Halmoni?" Yong Tu asked when his grandmother had finished her tale about the Korean alphabet. "How shall I ever learn enough to pass the Emperor's examinations?"

"You must study and study until you become as wise as your father, my Dragon Head. Kim Hong Chip passed the examinations at the very first try, for his learning was great and his verses were written with a dragon's brush. Your father deserved to win that contest of learning. When he set it to paper, his brush moved along with the speed of galloping horses. Some men there are who are given the *paksa's* hat for another reason than that of pure learning. Perhaps it is because they are good, or because they have our Jade Emperor's interest, like the young man who loved his father so much in the old tale, 'The Mourner Who Sang and the Nun Who Danced.'"

The children looked doubtful. They could not believe that such things could happen. The mourners they knew went about crying, *"Ai-go! Ai-go!"* In their coarse gray mourners' gowns and their mushroom-shaped mourners' hats, and with their little cotton face shields, they did not look as though they would ever wish to sing again.

And a nun who danced! Yong Tu and Ok Cha had seen these Buddhist nuns. They could tell them by their long yellow robes, but more easily by their closely shaven heads and their downcast eyes. How could it be that such a nun would dance?

"*Yé*, my doves, the mourner sang and the shaven-headed girl danced," Halmoni insisted. "You are no more surprised than was the King who looked in through the window and saw them. That one was a good king, too. Perhaps he was the very same king who gave us our alphabet. For his greatest care also was to make life better for his people.

"It was the custom of this King to dress himself as a farmer and trudge over the countryside to find out how his subjects were faring. One night he came to a poor hut from which came the sound of merry singing. Curious, the King entered the gate. Softly he crept near enough to look in through a peephole in the paper window-pane.

"To his amazement, the King saw an old man sadly weeping, while a mourner sang and a nun danced before him. It was the young man in the mourner's garb who answered the King's knock.

"'Good sir,' said the King, 'my lantern has gone out. May I rekindle its flame by your honorable fire?'

"'I pray the venerable gentleman to enter my humble

The mourners they knew went about crying, "Ai-go! Ai-go!" . . . they did not look as though they would ever wish to sing again.

house,' the mourner replied, and he hastened to perform the service the stranger requested.

" 'If I do not seem too curious,' the visitor said, 'could you explain these three mysteries to me? Why is it that an old man weeps, while a mourner sings and a nun dances before him?'

" 'Perhaps the gentleman will tell me first why he pries into the affair of another man's courts,' the young mourner said, annoyed at the questions of his strange guest.

" 'Forgive me. It is not just rude curiosity,' the King replied politely. 'I ask for a purpose, young sir. If you will enlighten my ignorance, good may come of it.'

"The King's words and kind manner impressed the young man. 'Hunger has long lived under our roof,' he explained. 'Our kitchen is empty. No ant is tempted to crawl upon its floor looking for crumbs. It is long since there was enough rice even to fill our own empty stomachs. Worst of all, we have not been able to find proper food for our aged father. Each day my sister has sold a strand of her hair to get a few cash with which to buy him a little bean soup. This very night her last lock was cut off. That is why her head now is close-shaven, and why she looks like a nun.

" 'My father, whose mind is not so clear as once it was, thinks she has become a nun to save him from starving. For that reason he weeps. And it is to stop his weeping that I sing and she dances. I wear my mourner's robe still though my mother has been dead far longer than the appointed three years. *Ai*, there is no money in our cash chests with which to buy other garments.'

"The King's heart was touched. He looked around the

poor hut, seeking a way in which to help this good son, and his eyes fell on a fine poem hanging upon the wall.

" 'Those words are golden,' he said, pointing to the wall writing. 'From whose brush do they come?'

" 'They are my own poor verses, honorable gentleman,' the young man said modestly. 'I have some learning, but I lack money for brushes, for ink, and for paper.'

" 'Your goodness to your father deserves a handsome reward, and such reward you shall have,' the King said to the young man in the gray mourner's dress. 'I can see you are well schooled. Present yourself at the Royal Examination Halls two days from now. There will be a place reserved for you.' And when he departed, he left behind money for food and for buying the rabbit-hair brush, the ink paste, and some paper.

"Now it was not the time of year for a King's Examination. Nor had one been planned. The scholars of the Capital shook their heads in amazement when the word was given out that such a contest of learning would take place in two days.

"They were even more puzzled at the subject that was announced. 'Whoever heard of writing an essay with such a title?' they complained to one another. 'An Old Man Weeps! A Mourner Sings! A Nun Dances!'

"The poor young man, still in his mourner's dress, was the only one who could give meaning to such a theme. In excellent verse he quickly set down the story he had told his curious visitor. And he was the first to throw his scroll over the fence of lances that surrounded the judges' court.

"The King declared him the winner of the contest of learning and called him to his palace. On his knees before the King, the young man bowed his head to the floor, after the custom of the Court.

" 'Do you not know me, excellent *paksa?*' the King asked him kindly.

" 'You are the King,' the trembling youth managed to say.

" 'I am also your curious visitor who came in the night,' the King replied. And with his own jade fingers he placed the *paksa's* hat on the young man's head. He called for fine clothes to replace the gray mourner's robe, and he hung the seal of Court office on the young man's belt. He ordered a court musician to lead his triumphal march through the city. A courtier ran ahead of him bearing the beribboned scrolls that told of his great honor.

"Clad in his silken coat and seated upon a white horse, the good son rode home in state to tell the news of his good fortune to his old father. Never again did the Spirit of Hunger fly inside their gate. Good fortune followed him and his sister. Go-betweens, offering her rich, handsome husbands, flocked to their gate. Thus was their goodness to their old father rewarded, as almost always happens, my son."

THE ANT
THAT
LAUGHED
TOO
MUCH

O<small>K CHA</small> and Halmoni were laughing. All the others, grownups and children, were laughing, too. Their olive-skinned faces were crinkled with smiles, and their narrow, almond-shaped eyes twinkled with fun. The Inner Court rang with the sound of their merriment.

The cause of it all was Yong Tu. He was trying to stand on his head as he had seen the funny acrobats do at the fair in the city the day before. It had been a splendid fair, with clowns and ropedancers, and tumblers who could do many more tricks than turning themselves thus upside down. Yong Tu could imitate the antics of the clowns, but he had no strong straw track, high up in the air, on which to try the ropedancing. It was perhaps a good thing, for he was having enough difficulty on the ground, pretending to be a traveling tumbler.

The boy's long braid of black hair kept getting in his way, until Halmoni loaned him a woman's hairpin to fasten the braid up on the crown of his head. This made his sister Ok Cha laugh louder than ever. She laughed and laughed, until her very sides ached.

"Take care, Jade Child," her grandmother warned her. "Take care, or like the ant that laughed too much, you will meet with disaster."

"What happened to the ant, Halmoni?" the little girl asked, with one eye still on Yong Tu. He had tired of trying to get his feet up into the air and was now rolling about on the ground, playing with Dog.

"You shall hear, blessed girl," the old grandmother said, hoping to calm the giggling child. "This ant was a wise old ant and greatly respected in the garden where she lived. Everyone came to her for advice, and so it was not at all strange that the earthworm should choose her to act as a go-between and find him a wife.

" 'I badly want a good wife, Omoni,' the earthworm said to the ant. 'Someone who will take care of my clothes and prepare my rice and *kimchee*. Find me a young wife, a healthy and strong one. I know you will choose wisely.'

"The ant agreed, and she was thinking over the problem one sunny afternoon, when she met a strong, healthy centipede.

" 'How would you like to become a bride?' the ant asked the young centipede.

" 'Well enough! Well enough!' was the centipede's reply. 'But you must tell me first about the bridegroom.'

" 'The bridegroom is industrious. He is calm. He is patient,' the ant replied with enthusiasm.

It was a splendid fair, with clowns and dancers who ran along straw ropes high up in the air.

" 'Does he live in this garden?' the centipede asked.

" '*Yé*, he lives in this garden, though often he is out of sight of those who walk on its paths.'

" 'That is true of all garden creatures,' the centipede said. 'Tell me more about the bridegroom.'

" 'Well, he is many times longer than you, and he moves about well, although he has no legs.'

" 'That would be a fine centipede,' the prospective bride said with scorn. 'What kind of husband for me would be one without any legs?'

" 'He is an honorable earthworm,' the ant then confessed.

" '*Ai*, a damp, clammy earthworm!' The centipede shook her head. 'An earthworm would never do. His body reaches too far. I should never have patience enough to make a coat for such a long creature.'

"The ant thought this very funny. She laughed and she laughed as she scurried down the garden path to tell the bad news to the waiting bridegroom.

" '*Ai*, Earthworm,' she said between her fits of laughter. 'I found a young bride, a beautiful centipede, healthy and strong, but she will have none of you. She says she will never have a husband without any legs. She says you are too long. She would never have patience enough to sew up your clothes.' And the ant went off into fits of laughter again.

" 'I do not find this joke funny,' the earthworm said indignantly. 'Why should a centipede laugh at a fine earthworm like me? I would not have her either. With all those legs of hers! No! Again, no! How should I ever get enough straw to make shoes for so many feet? The bargain is off.'

"Well, the ant thought this even funnier than the remarks of the centipede. She laughed and she laughed until her sides ached. She feared she would burst. So she took a straw rope and tied herself tightly together about her middle.

"Only when she had forgotten about her adventures as go-between for the earthworm and the centipede, did the ant untie the rope. And what do you think had happened, Ok Cha?" The grandmother paused for a moment, enjoying the little girl's eager, questioning face.

"That ant had laughed too much. Her waist was so firmly pinched in by the straw rope that it never grew large again. Remember this story, Ok Cha, the next time you meet an ant on the path in our Garden of Green Gems. Then you will understand why that ant's waist is so small."

RICE

FROM

A

CAT'S

FUR

Almost every day beggars knocked at the bamboo gate of the wealthy Kim family. When Dog's barking brought Old Pak, the gatekeeper, out to greet them, they pleaded, "Will the Gentleman of this House spare us a few grains of rice from his great store? Our rice bowls are empty. We have tasted nothing but grass roots and the bark off the trees for many days."

Yong Tu's curiosity took him into the entrance court almost every time Dog gave warning of such visitors.

"Their clothes are in rags, Halmoni," he would report. "Their hair is uncombed. Their faces are thin. They look very hungry. The children are crying."

Ok Cha would then gaze eagerly up at their grandmother. She knew well the tender-hearted woman would give her usual order that rice be provided for these poor hungry people.

"Why are there so many more beggars now than at any other time of the year, Halmoni?" Ok Cha asked one afternoon when Yong Tu had returned from taking some rice out to the bamboo gate.

"It's the time of the 'Spring Suffering,' precious Jade

Child," was the old woman's answer. "At this season few in our land have much rice left in their storerooms. Under many a grass roof hunger comes each year with the Spring. The grain stored for the Winter then is all eaten. The new rice or millet plants are only just starting to shoot their green spears up through the earth. There is nothing yet in the gardens. Many families have not enough cash in their money chests with which to buy rice. They never taste meat or fish. They can't even afford to buy an old dog from the dog-meat shop."

"What do those poor people do, Halmoni?" Ok Cha asked, her narrow, dark eyes filling with tears.

"Why, they eat grass roots and bark, my child, just as those beggars said yesterday. And perhaps luckier people help them as we do. Or else some good spirit rides on the wind to their aid." The grandmother noticed the distress in the child's eyes, and she wanted to comfort her. "Perhaps they find a magic cat like the one whose fur dripped rice in the old story."

"That would be good, Halmoni," Ok Cha said eagerly. "Did that truly happen?"

"*Ai*, child, what does it matter whether it really happened? Who can say it did not? I like to think that it did, for the people in this story were good people. They did not deserve to be hungry.

"Many hundreds of years ago, perhaps even a thousand, there lived in our country a good scholar named Yo. What his other names were I have forgotten, but they were not important. So wise a scholar was this Yo that his fame spread over the land, even to the ears of the King himself.

" 'Send for that Scholar Yo,' the King commanded. 'He

shall give us his wise counsel. He shall have a post at our court. He shall have the right to wear the precious peacock feather in his hat.'

"Now Yo was a kind man as well as a man of great learning. While the other ministers grew rich in their office, Yo seemed to grow poor. So busy was he in his great position at Court that he gave no thought to his own affairs. His three daughters, who looked after his house, often found no rice in the storeroom. Their father had thoughtlessly given it all to the beggars who came to his gate.

"That was in a time when our Little Kingdom badly needed the help of its elder brother, China. Who could better be sent to persuade the Emperor on that Dragon Throne than wise Minister Yo? The journey was long. The men who would carry Yo's traveling chair could go no faster then than such men go today. Full three years would pass before Yo could return from his mission to China.

" 'Ai-go! Ai-go! What shall we do?' Yo's daughters wept when their father announced his departure. 'We have but one dress apiece, Abuji. Two of us must wash the dress of the other. She must remain hidden under the coverlids until we have brought it out from under the ironing sticks. We manage badly. There is but one jar of rice left in our storeroom. How shall we eat when you are gone and there is no one to put more cash in our money box?'

"Now in this household the favorite pet of the Master was a clever black cat. Not wild like the cats we know, Ok Cha, but gentle and loving! When Yo bent over his books in his Hall of Perfect Learning, the cat lay in his lap. It purred and it purred while the man rubbed the soft fur just under its chin. One strange thing about this cat was that it never closed its eyes. No one had ever caught it asleep. It just lay still, purred and purred, and watched over the household.

" 'Of course you will eat, my daughters,' Yo said, as he climbed into his traveling chair. 'Heaven will care for you while I am gone. And if your rice should give out, and there should be no other way, turn to my black cat. Rub his fur carefully in this fashion.' The man ran his slim fingers through the soft fur of the cat, which had jumped into his lap. He began at its tail, and he stroked its fur towards its head. Then he gently handed the black cat down into the arms of one of his daughters.

"The girls did not love the black cat so dearly as did their father, and I am afraid they forgot these parting words. As long as the rice in their storeroom held out, they managed to live. But they ate only nine times in a month, and always they were hungry. Now, even the largest jar becomes empty at last, my children, and the day came when there was no rice at all in their kitchen.

" 'We must sell our belongings,' the sisters cried sadly. Fine chests bound with brass, handsome embroidered silks, even their treasured hairpins of silver and coral, had to be sold to give them money for rice. But that too was eaten. Soon their house was as empty as the rice jars in the storeroom.

" 'What was it our father said about the black cat?' one sister then asked the others.

The Emperor gave Yo a post at his court and the right to wear the precious peacock feather in his hat.

" 'Perhaps he spoke a riddle which will help us get food,' another sister suggested.

" 'If only we could remember what he said about the black cat!' the third one cried.

"That evening, as they sat hungry in their Inner Chamber, the black cat jumped into the lap of the youngest girl 'It was this way we should rub his fur. Now I remember!' she cried suddenly, and she began to run her fingers gently along the cat's soft furry back from his tail to his head. Some call this rubbing a cat's fur the wrong way, but for them it proved to be the right way.

" '*Hé! Hai! Hai!*' they all cried. 'Rice drips from the cat's fur!'

"It was true! Before their very eyes a steady stream of rice grains dripped from the fur of their father's black cat. Fine, whole grains they were, white as the snow of winter, clean and smooth enough for the cooking pot. The more the girl rubbed the cat's fur, the more rice showered from it. It made a great mound upon the clean floor.

"Laughter and rejoicing filled Yo's house that evening. Once more his daughters' stomachs were full, and the days ahead seemed as rosy and fair as the rising sun. Never would they be hungry again, no matter how long their father tarried.

"The sisters took turns in rubbing the black cat's soft fur. When they had more rice than they needed to fill their own rice jars, they sold it for much money. Now they could buy back their fine brassbound chests, their handsome embroideries, and their precious hairpins of coral and silver. Now they could buy cloth for new dresses, and even black oil to make their hair neat and shining. If they had wished, they could have had an Ancestors' Feast every day of the year.

"At the end of three years Yo returned from the court of the Chinese Emperor with his mission accomplished. As soon as he had greeted his daughters, he called for his black cat. When he heard how the magic rice had dripped out of its fur to save them from starving, he said, 'Now I am home again. I have secured for the King the aid our land needs from China. My reward will be great. Our cash chest will overflow. Never will our food jars be empty again. Nevermore shall we need to rub rice from our cat's fur.'

"And never again did it happen, my dear ones. Secretly the youngest girl tried rubbing the cat's fur from its tail to its head. But the cat only purred and purred and watched over the household through his wide-open eyes."

THE

BEGGARS'

FRIEND

THE white-clad Korean grandmother looked anxiously up at the dark clouds racing across the heavens above her.

"The rain comes, blessed ones," she warned the children in the Inner Court. "Hurry, like the crickets, into the house!"

The boys and girls scarcely heard her, so intent were they on the games they were playing on the hard-packed earth of the Inner Court. Ok Cha and two of her small cousins were sitting with their legs tucked under their full gay-colored skirts. They were busy with *tja-si*, or jackstones. Instead of metal jacks, however, these small girls were tossing and picking up the thick Korean pennies, called "cash." Ok Cha had safely got through "laying the eggs" and "setting the eggs," but she missed the third toss when she tried to knock on the ground in "hatching the eggs."

Yong Tu and the other boys also were playing a game with these dark metal coins made of copper and brass. They were "hitting the cash," throwing one coin at another placed in the center of a square drawn on the ground. The boys did not mind losing a cash or two to one another. These coins were worth little, only a fraction as much as a penny of the United States.

Suddenly the dark clouds over their heads began to send huge drops of rain down on the young players. Although their grandmother's words had gone unheeded, the boys and girls jumped at this direct warning. Like startled chickens, they rushed up the veranda steps to take shelter within the old woman's room.

And just in time, too, for now the clouds seemed to open and great sheets of water were drenching the earth. It was the midsummer season of the Great Rains. Almost every day floods like this descended from the clouded sky.

"All my cash are gone but these two!" Yong Tu lamented, running the lonely coins back and forth along his cash string of braided straw. Everyone in Korea carried his cash on such strings, which were run through the square holes punched in the coins' centers. The strings of cash in this family's huge money chests were heavy and long. It took a sturdy servant, or even a pony, to carry enough cash to buy the family supplies in the city market.

"You should have a magic cash string, like that of Woo, the beggars' friend," Halmoni said to the boy. "That string never grew less. Sit down and wait until the rain has passed by, and I'll tell you about it."

The children all gathered about their beloved grandmother. And while they nibbled contentedly at the pine nuts and honey candy she brought forth, she told them the tale.

"The man in this story was a spoonmaker named Woo,

who lived in a modest house in the Street of Spoonmakers here in our city. Woo was a kind husband and a good father. There were always bundles of grass for mending holes in his roof. There was always fresh rice straw to make sandals for his children's feet. And there were always rice and *kimchee* in the brown jars in his court.

"This Woo had a heart as big as the sky, my precious ones. Of course, when his children were small and needed clothing and food, he took care of them first. But when his son was grown up and his daughters were married, he began to give more and more to the beggars who knocked at the gate of his spoonmaking shop. It was a bowl of rice to this one, and a few cash to that one. Now a few cash will not buy a coat or a pig, but if you put enough raindrops together you have a river. And like a river, cash flowed out of Woo's money chests into the outstretched hands of these hungry beggars.

"How those miserable fellows fought to get to their friend, Woo the Spoonmaker! The man had to take only one step out of his gate, and they came running. Night after night he returned to his home without one coin in the belt pocket his good wife had embroidered for him.

"At last there was no cash at all left in his money chests. There was nothing with which to buy rice for his eating bowls, nor brass to make shining spoons which might have brought him new money. As happens to many, Woo began to borrow. And as happens also to those who do not pay back what they borrow, he was hauled before the judge.

"There he was soundly paddled, and it was only when the jailers found out Woo had nothing to give them that they let him go. It was a bruised, beaten Woo, a sad, sorry spoonmaker, that limped through the muddy streets to his poor home again.

"Woo was just entering his gate when the toe of his sandal tripped upon something hard. Looking down in the dirt to see what it could be, Woo found a straw string on which were strung seven pieces of cash.

" 'Seven cash are not many, but they will buy us at least some rice for our supper,' Woo said to his sad wife. And he sent his son out to bring back the good grain.

"Now here the wonder took place. Woo had picked off five of the coins to give to his son. Yet when he looked down at the string, there were still seven cash on it. He could not believe his eyes. He called his good wife to come and count the coins also. He pulled off four more coins; still seven remained. When Woo lay down on the floor to sleep that night, the riddle still puzzled him. He rose again and again to test the cash string. No matter how many times he pulled coins off of its end, always seven were left.

" 'Thus is goodness rewarded,' his wife said to Woo. And they hid their magic string of cash well, saying no word of its powers.

"Bright shining spoons now were made again in Woo's house on the Street of the Spoonmakers. So if the neighbors wondered about the new roof on his house and the fine new hat the man wore, they could think they were bought with money his customers paid him.

"Now Woo's great heart was still as big as the sky, and he still gave to the poor. But he made his gifts in secret now, lest the judge and the jailers should drag him back to the prison. Instead of strewing money about through the crowds on the streets, he made journeys into the country, tossing a few cash through the dogholes in the gates of poor families. Or he went even farther into the hills to the temple of the Great Buddha. There he gave strings of cash to the good priests for their poor boxes.

"At this same time, my children, there were puzzled faces in the Royal Treasure House here in the Capital. 'How can it be that so much money disappears?' the King's Treasurer asked his assistants.

"All shook their heads. Each one knew how many coins he himself had slipped into his pocket, as his proper 'squeeze.' You know what a 'squeeze' is, I am sure. You've often heard your father complain of officials who take for themselves a fat share of the taxes the people pay to the King. Well, that is a squeeze.

"But many more coins than their squeeze had vanished. Who could be the thief? The assistants stood guard while the King's Treasurer watched.

"One morning at daybreak the Treasurer heard a sharp, clinking sound on the tops of the piles of cash. To his amazement, several coins rose into the air and flew out through a hole in the Treasury roof. Off they went, by twos and by threes, by fours and by fives. Each time Woo pulled cash off his magic string, coins were whisked away. By closely watching, the Treasurer could see them riding the wind to the roof of Woo's little house.

"The good *tokgabi* who had put the magic string at Woo's gate gave the spoonmaker warning before the Treasury guards came to get him.

" 'Take our precious cash string with you and hide it well,' Woo said to his wife. 'Make your way to the temple of the Great Buddha. The good priests will give us shelter. Wait there till I come!'

"With their son his wife set out at once for the faraway temple on the Diamond Mountain. The cash string was safely tucked away, far inside her sleeve.

"The Treasury guards came, and Woo was again brought before the Judge. But this time there was no mention of paddling. A man who knew such a secret as his was far too important to be beaten to death. 'Perhaps,' the Judge thought, 'this spoonmaker can be persuaded to bring money through the air into my pocket, too.'

"Now Woo had no intention of parting with the secret of his magic cash string. And he knew he must find a way to make his escape before the Judge put him in jail, where the locks were strong and the paddles were like iron.

" 'Honorable Judge,' this spoonmaker said craftily, 'I will indeed show you the secret of my coins that ride on the wind. But it will take time. I need a great sheet of paper, some ink and an inkstone, and a rabbit-hair pen.'

"The large sheet of paper was pasted upon a broad screen, and with the hair pen Woo began to draw black lines upon it. The attendants gaped as they saw appear, there before their very eyes, a donkey, life-size. The little round eyes, the stiff hairy mane, the tiny neat hoofs, the long tufted tail one after another, each part of the donkey's body came into being under Woo's brush.

" 'I must not work too fast. My wife must have a good start,' Woo thought to himself, and he took great pains in drawing the nose and the mouth of the donkey. The courtiers began to laugh and to whisper, 'It looks just like the Judge.'

" 'But it has only one ear,' one onlooker said.

" 'That's like the Judge, too. He never hears but one side

of a case,' another declared. And they fell to laughing louder and louder.

"The Judge, hearing their merriment, came to look at the donkey himself. Straightway he flew into a rage, for he, too, saw the likeness. 'Bring out the paddles,' cried the angry official. But Woo quickly brushed in the other ear, and the picture was finished.

"At once the paper donkey began to move its head. With a loud heehaw a live animal trotted right out of the screen. Woo leaped on its back, and the donkey galloped away. Across the courtyard and out of the open gate it went before the astonished guards could stop it. And that was the last those people ever saw of Woo, the beggars' friend."

"What became of him, Halmoni?" Yong Tu asked the story-teller.

"Did he catch up with his wife?" Ok Cha wanted to know.

"That he did, little precious," the Korean grandmother answered. "And though the people of Seoul never saw Woo again, still they heard much about him. The beggars followed him to his new home in the Temple of the Great Buddha on the Diamond Mountain. And they received from the priests there alms which Woo provided. So long as Woo lived, cash from the Royal Treasure House still rode on the winds to refill his magic string.

"When Woo finally died, some say the Court Treasurers neglected to mention it to the King. They only took more and more 'squeeze' for themselves, and they still blamed it on Woo and his magic cash string. The piles of money in the Treasury grew smaller year after year.

"Then a wiser king came to sit on our Dragon Throne.

One day he hid his jade person under a beggar's robe. He went to seek Woo himself at the Temple of the Great Buddha. To that king's surprise, he found the temple in ruins and he learned Woo had died many, many years since. From that time on, not nearly so much money flew out of the Royal Treasury into the pockets of dishonest officials.

THE

VILLAGE

OF

THE PURE

QUEEN

THE great bell of Seoul spoke to the men of the city each evening about nine o'clock. At that hour the bellmen thrust the huge, hanging beam against its metal sides, and its booming notes sounded through all the streets of the Capital. "All men indoors! Lock the seven city gates! Clear the streets so that women may safely leave the inner courts!" This was the message which "Man Guide," as the bell was called, gave out with its thundering voice.

"There are rough men in our land, just as there are in other lands," Halmoni said to Ok Cha. "Tales are told of bold ones who carry off brides from the very gates of their houses. When men are abroad, women are safe only inside their own inner court."

That is why none but servant maids, singing girls, and those in from the country were seen in the streets of Seoul in the daytime. That is why, so Halmoni said, a wise king had long ago ordered the custom of ringing the men into their houses when evening came. With the streets empty, and under the shelter of darkness, it was quite safe for women then to walk abroad to pay visits. They might even go to buy in the shops the things peddlers had not yet brought to their gates.

When Ok Cha's mother and the other women of the Kim household walked out of the bamboo gate, each one threw over her head a long, bright green silken coat. With its sleeves flapping empty about her shoulders, she drew it together over her face, so that only one eye peeped out. Safely hidden thus, she would be mistaken for an ordinary woman. No one would guess she belonged to a rich family like the Kims.

"There's a story about those green coats," Halmoni once told Ok Cha. "Earlier they were men's garments. Then there was a war. A beautiful princess escaped from the enemy by throwing her father's green coat over her head and covering her face with it. That proved what a good protection it was. Ever since, the women of Seoul have worn such a coat during their walks on the streets."

Ok Cha liked to go out into the city with her mother and the maidservant who carried the lantern. She learned to pick her way carefully amid the dirt and the holes in the narrow unpaved streets. At the same time she could see

Ok Cha's mother threw over her head a long, bright green silken coat for her walks outside the bamboo gate.

all the interesting things about which Yong Tu and the men of her family talked so much.

The part of the city the little girl liked the best was that called Chung-dong, or the Village of the Pure Queen. There could be seen the curving roofs of the Emperor's palace, the only building in Seoul which rose more than one story above the ground. It would not be fitting, Halmoni said, that other buildings should be taller and perhaps look down on the courts of their Jade Ruler. Ok Cha was always a little afraid of the statues of the Flame Swallowers which protected the palace from fire. These were two monsters in stone which would surely eat up the fire spirits before they could enter the royal gates. With all the houses of the palace attendants, and with the many temples near by, Ok Cha thought that Chung-dong was far more like a town than like a village.

"Who was the Pure Queen, Halmoni?" the little girl asked one morning, following an evening excursion into the city with her mother and the other women of the Inner Court.

"*Hé*, that person was a good person, and a wise one, too. They say that she was called Kang and that she was only a simple girl who lived far out in the country. One evening when Kang was drawing water up from the village well, a fine general rode up on horseback. He was an important man, as one could see by the number of servants who ran by his side and by the number of soldiers who formed his bodyguard. But great ones and lesser ones are much the same, Jade Child, when it comes to being thirsty and tired.

"The day was hot, and the journey had been long. The General's face was the color of a red peony bloom. Beads of water made tiny brooks that trickled down his broad cheeks. 'Give me water to drink,' the General said to the girl, when he had given her polite greeting.

"The girl Kang bowed in return, and she filled a big bowl of water, freshly drawn from the well. But before she handed the bowl up to the great man, she plucked a number of tender green willow leaves and dropped them into the cold water.

"The General took the bowl in his hands and began to drink. He was greatly annoyed when he found how the willow leaves got in his way. Instead of taking the huge gulps, which his thirst called for, he was forced to sip slowly.

"When he had drained the big bowl at last, the General scolded the girl; but he spoke gently, because she was in truth of a jade prettiness.

" 'It was not very polite of this young person to throw leaves into my drinking bowl,' the General said to Kang.

" 'It was only because I feared for the health of the Great General,' the young girl replied. 'You were overheated and tired, honorable sir. With quick drinking you would have swallowed the spirits of sickness. You might even have died. It was to prevent this that I put the willow leaves into the bowl. They forced you to drink slowly with very small sips. Thus no harm could come to you.'

"The General said to himself, 'This maid is as wise as she is beautiful. There is love for her in my heart.' Then he said to the girl, 'I will make you my bride if you will but wait until the war ends.'

"Well, my children, the girl waited, and at last that war was over. When Kang's bridegroom came riding upon his white horse, who should he be but this very same General. And who should that general have been but the famous General Yi, who later became King of our Dragon Backed Country. It is a son of this Yi family who dwells in the Jade Palace of our land today.

"Now, of course, the King had many other wives also in his palace, as do all kings," Halmoni went on with her tale. "But they say he admired none as he admired his good Queen Kang. Her wisdom shed light upon his most troublesome problems of state, and he always consulted her.

"No doubt she even had a voice in choosing the place for this city of Seoul. Her sedan chair was carried just behind the chair of the King when this valley in the mountains was selected for his new capital. We know she had a voice in choosing her own grave site.

" 'When I have mounted the Dragon, you must build a huge kite and write my name *Kang* upon it,' the good Queen said to the King. 'Let the wind take the kite high into the air above the Royal Palace. Then do you break the string. Where the kite falls, there let my spirit rest.'

"So it was done, precious girl. The King himself sent the huge kite up into the sky. With his own jade fingers he cut its string. Like a great wounded butterfly, the kite slowly fluttered down to the earth. On the little ridge where it landed, Queen Kang's tomb was built.

" 'The Pure Tomb,' it was called. For many years it remained there, close to the Palace. The sad King liked to listen to the music of the bells in the little temple above it. He thought they were like the soft voice of his departed Queen Kang.

"Another king of that family moved this tomb later to

the eastern edge of the city. More and more houses were built upon its former site so near the Palace. But the people did not forget the wisdom and goodness of their former Queen Kang. They called that place, as we still do, the 'Village of the Pure Queen.'"

A

STORY

FOR

SALE

ONE hot summer afternoon Halmoni and her grand-children were sitting, pleasantly idle, beside the cool sparkling brook in the Garden of Green Gems. They were talking of this and of that, of nothing in particular. As usual at such times, one of the children said, "Tell us a story, Halmoni, a new story, one we've not heard before."

"How much will you pay for a story?" the Korean grand-mother asked teasingly.

None of these children thought such a question strange. Traveling poets often knocked at the Kim gate and asked if the Master would not buy a poem from them. Did not the traveling storytellers at the market and the fairs always demand pay for the good tales they told there? Even their own poet-father received pay for his verses. But of course his pay was in gifts of fat roasted chickens, of bolts of grass linen, or of a new finely sewn collar for his silken coat. These gifts to him were tokens of admiration from friends —even from strangers—for the golden words that flowed from his rabbit-hair brush.

"How much would your story cost, Halmoni?" Ok Cha said, coming close and laying her hand affectionately on the old woman's shoulder.

"Well, I don't know." The Korean grandmother smiled. "Yi and his wife paid a full hundred strings of cash for a story. They really got no story at all though, in the end, it turned out to be worth a great deal of money to them.

"We'll talk about the price some other time," Halmoni continued. "And I'll tell you about this story Old Yi bought at such a great price. Yi was a rich fellow who lived with his wife far out in the country and far up on a hillside. They had many times a hundred strings of cash in their house. So much did they have, indeed, that their brass-bound chests overflowed, and they hid part of their wealth in the great *kimchee* jars, buried deep in their courtyard.

"Riches do not always bring pleasure, my little ones. There were no sons in that house far up on the hillside, and no grandchildren to bother." Halmoni smiled so that her listeners knew she did not mean the last words just as they sounded. "No, it was as still as the ancestors' tomb under Yi's roof. The old couple often were lonely. Traveling actors or storytellers never knocked at their gate, so far off the road. They were too old to go in their sedan chairs to pay visits or find amusement at the town fairs. Today was like tomorrow, and the evenings were long.

"One morning the Master of that house called Hap, his

gatekeeper, to him. 'Go down to the valley,' he commanded, 'and do not stop walking until you have found a good storyteller. Buy from him a fine tale. You can pay him one hundred strings of cash for it!'

"This gatekeeper, Hap, was a dark, ignorant fellow. He himself would not have known a storyteller from a woodcutter. But he loaded the chest containing the cash on a wooden carrying frame, which we call a jiggy. He raised this up on his back. Then he trotted off down the hillside in search of a fine tale to bring back to his master.

"Many hours Hap walked along the path through the valley before he met anyone. Then he came on a farmer, resting by the side of a stream that ran through some rice fields.

" 'Have you been in peace, venerable sir?' Hap said, bowing in polite greeting.

" '*Yé*, Uncle, and you, have you eaten your honorable meals?' the stranger returned his courtesy, according to custom.

" 'Will the Learned Man tell me if he has a story which he will sell? My Master has ordered me to buy a fine tale.'

"Now this stranger was but a countryman himself, a man also without learning. He had no story on his tongue's tip, nor could he remember one. But he had great need of money, and he did not wish to let such a good chance slip by.

" '*Yé*, Uncle, I have a story,' he said to the gatekeeper. 'But it will cost a large sum. How much can your Master pay?'

" 'Will a hundred strings of cash be enough? That is all I have in this money box.'

The farmer was overjoyed when he heard of this goodly sum, and he nodded his head. He thought hard, for he still could remember no story and he had not the wits to invent one. As he gazed about him in his need, he saw a long-legged stork, picking its way through the rice field. Daintily lifting first one leg and then the other, the great bird moved towards the stream.

" 'He comes! Step by step!' The farmer spoke aloud. 'Step by step he comes nearer.' And the stupid gatekeeper, thinking the man was beginning the story, repeated his words. He must know this fine tale by heart so that he could tell it to the Master.

" 'He comes! Step by step!' Hap echoed. 'Step by step he comes nearer!'

"At that moment the stork saw a movement in the rice, and he halted to find out just what it was. 'Now he stops to listen! Now he stops to look!' the farmer said with his eyes still on the stork.

" 'Now he stops to listen! Now he stops to look!' the gatekeeper chanted.

"The rice plants no longer moved, and the stork bent his neck to hunt for some good morsel, an earthworm or perhaps a snail on the ground. With bent legs and slow steps the bird crept through the field.

" 'He bends down! He creeps!' the farmer went on, hoping that the stork would furnish him with a satisfactory tale. And the gatekeeper spoke likewise, reciting each word with great care.

"Then there was a quick movement in the rice, and a fox raised its black nose out of the green. With a leap off the ground the stork spread its broad wings and flew quickly to safety.

" '*Ai! Ai!*' cried the farmer. 'He's off! He is fleeing. Soon he will be safe!'

" 'He's off. He is fleeing. Soon he will be safe!' his listener cried too.

" 'Is that all the story?' Hap asked the stranger when no more words came from his lips.

" 'That is all. Who could want more?' the farmer said haughtily, and he loaded Hap's hundred strings of cash on his own 'jiggy.'

"On his way home up the hillside, Hap repeated this story over and over. He was proud that he did not forget one single word. Of course he did not understand it, but then he was a dark, unlearned fellow.

"Old Yi and his wife also thought it a queer tale. They did not understand it, either. The old man told it over aloud night after night, trying to puzzle out its meaning.

"Now in that lonely region, it is not at all strange that one evening a wicked man came to rob this rich aged couple. The robber was young, and it was no trouble to him to climb over the wall. With soft steps the thief was making his way toward the house, when he heard a voice say, 'He comes! Step by step! Step by step he comes nearer.'

"This brought the thief to a standstill. 'The Master of this House does not see me. How can he know I am here?' he thought to himself. And he held his breath, listening and looking about him.

"The voice came again. 'Now he stops to listen! Now he stops to look!'

"The thief could not understand how the man inside the house knew just what he was doing. But he was bold, and he began to creep toward the light that shone through the window paper.

" 'He bends down! He creeps!' The voice of Yi, telling the story to his old wife, came clearer and clearer.

" 'How can he know each thing I do?' the robber thought. He began to be frightened. 'This must be the house of a spirit,' he said to himself. 'I had best get out of here.'

"And as he turned to run away, the voice of Old Yi followed him. 'He's off,' it cried. 'Soon he will be safe!'

"And that thief ran as fast as ever he could, leaping the wall at the very first try and never stopping until he reached his brother thieves in the town down in the valley.

"All those wicked men shook their heads at the tale their frightened friend told them. And none of them ever again tried to rob the house of Old Yi who bought the farmer's story for a hundred strings of cash!"

THE

TWO

STONE

GIANTS

Dog was barking, and servants were rushing this
way and that in the Outer Court. Old Pak had
run to open the bamboo gate, and Yong Tu and
his cousins raced around the corner of the Hall of Perfect
Learning. The Master of the House was returning from his
journey to Songdo, the old High Tree Capital, far to the
north. His traveling chair was already in sight down the
street.

The sedan chair bearers in their blue suits and red sashes
trotted in through the bamboo gate. They seemed as fresh
as if they had not borne their master many miles over the
rough Korean country roads. Kim Hong Chip rose from his
seat on the floor of the little curtained box which they had
set down on the ground. He stepped stiffly out between the
poles on which it was slung and walked across the hard-
packed earth of the courtyard. Even with changing his
position again and again, and with descending from the
chair to walk over smooth level parts of the roads, his legs
were cramped with his long journey.

"Bring the package to the Inner Court," Kim Hong Chip said to a servant. Then, followed by the children, he made his way to Halmoni's apartment to report his safe return.

The old woman's eyes sparkled with pleasure when the package disclosed two beautiful bowls of clear, sea-green porcelain. Songdo, once the capital and the center of Korean art, was famous for such delicate vases with their patterns wrought clearly under the gleaming green surface.

All the family gathered about the Master of the House when he had finished his evening meal. He was tired, and his wife had brought his eating table to him in Halmoni's room. No one spoke while the Master was dining, for in Korea then it was thought that talk spoiled the food. "Eat while you eat, and talk when you have finished," Halmoni taught her grandchildren.

"Tell us of your journey, great traveler," the old woman said when the brass rice spoon had been laid down and the chopsticks had been wiped clean of *kimchee* and put into their embroidered case.

"It was a good journey, and luck traveled with me," Kim Hong Chip began. "There were demon posts often along the way to frighten off the bad spirits. We took care to toss stones on the spirit piles under the trees. And I got down out of my chair to bow before the two great *miryeks*. These men of stone are very big, Omoni. They look very powerful. Bad spirits surely must fear them."

The man was speaking of two giant stone figures along the travel route between Korea's capital city, Seoul, and its former old High Tree Capital, Songdo. All through this land there are stone figures like these, which the people called *miryeks,* or men of stone. Smaller ones are the devil posts, set up to protect villages and roads from bad spirits which might be riding by on the winds. Others are great giants in stone, carved on the faces of the cliffs or out of some rocky point.

"Were those two *miryeks* as big as the White Buddha, Abuji?" Yong Tu asked his father. The boy once made a picnic journey with his family to see this Great White Buddha which is carved on a cliff a few miles from their city of Seoul. A stream ran at its foot. The country folk in the valley there say that no matter how great the floods are, water never touches the garments of this likeness of the wise teacher, Buddha. A little roof over its towering head keeps the rain and the sleet from washing the statue's white paint away too quickly.

"*Yé,* my son, these two *miryeks* are even taller than the White Buddha. Like a giant man and his wife, they stand side by side. A man and a woman they are, too, carved from great pointed rocks."

"There's a story about those two *miryeks,*" Halmoni said, thoughtfully. "They were built to drive away beggars, not spirits, so my grandmother said. And they did drive the beggars away, but not as their builder had planned."

"Now I recall that tale, too, Omoni," the old woman's son said. "Tell it to the children, as you told it to me when I was the age of Yong Tu."

"Well, those *miryeks* are not far from the place where a rich man once lived. He had a fine house with five different gates. I do not remember his name, but we may as well call him Yong. Yong's heart was kind, like that of Yo in the story of the Magic Cat. Like Woo, the Spoonmaker, he never could bring himself to turn beggars away from his gate.

"In processions the beggars came. Buddhist priests with their begging bowls and little brass bells; poor farmers whose rice plants had yielded no grain that year; even city folk from whom wicked officials had taken their last strings of cash—all these trod the well-worn path to Yong's open gates. The servants in that household were kept running back and forth from morning till night to put rice and cash into the outstretched hands of those beggars.

"But when water is always poured out of a bowl and none is poured in, the bowl soon is empty, my little dragons. So it was with Yong's cash chests. He became frightened at the lessening number of the coins on their bottoms.

"One afternoon a traveler knocked at the gate and asked if he might come in for a rest. This one was an old man, and he wore a poet's hat. Yong invited the aged scholar into his House of Guests. He offered him a bowl of hot rice and a cup of good wine to refresh him.

" 'Wisdom drips from your tongue, honorable sir,' Yong said to his visitor. 'Give me of your jade counsel. So many cash have I given away to the beggars who crowd my gate that my fortune soon will be gone. Yet I cannot bring myself to turn them away. What can I do?'

"The old man sat quiet, thinking. Then he spoke thus, 'It is very simple. If the Great Man will come out with me into the courtyard, I will show him the way.' There he pointed to two tall pillars of stone which jutted out of a cliff not far away. 'Make those two rocks into *miryeks*. Carve them into a giant man and a giant woman. When the great stone figures are completed, I promise you no more beggars will come to your gate.'

"When the old man had departed, Yong thought long over his words. 'Making *miryeks* would cost too much,' he said at first. But so many more beggars clamored for cash that he decided to follow the old man's advice.

"And the stone carving did cost much. It cost all the cash in all the rich man's money boxes. But finally the two giant *miryeks* stood there, as tall and as powerful as they look today. Each wore a stone hat on its head and stone robes on its shoulders.

"Not long thereafter the learned old traveler again called at Yong's gate. But Yong had no pleasant, polite words of welcome for him this time. He grabbed him by his gray topknot, and he shook him well. 'How dare you come back here again, Old Man?' he cried. 'You have brought ruin upon me, you and your *miryeks!*'

"But the old man only smiled and asked, 'Will the Great Man be pleased to have a little patience? What was the charm you asked of me?'

" 'I asked for a charm to keep beggars away.'

" 'And does this charm not work? I saw no beggars at your gate.'

"Yong looked crestfallen. 'No, there are no beggars there,' he admitted. 'They well know there is nothing here for them now.'

" 'Then you should not complain. I gave you the charm for which you asked. And you have learned what everyone else in this land knows—the only place where beggars are not is where there is nothing to be given away.'

"Yong bowed to the old man, begging his pardon. 'You

speak wise words again,' he said. 'It is I who have been foolish. But it would have been better for me to empty my money chests for poor hungry beggars rather than for those two people of stone.' "

THE

MOLE

AND

THE

MIRYEK

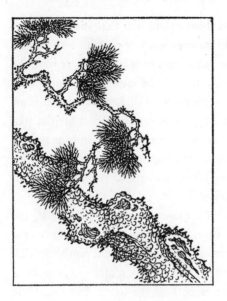

HALMONI knew another story about *miryeks*. She told it to Yong Tu one day in winter when he and the other boys were building a snow *miryek* out in the courtyard.

The white flakes had been falling and falling for several days, and the great mountains about Seoul rose in a vast white wall against the winter sky. The wind had been blowing during the night. There were deep drifts in the corners of the Inner Court, splendid for gathering by the handfuls to build up the figure of a snow man. The boys had worked well. Their snow *miryek* stood up very straight, as if it were proud of the old horsehair hat they set on its head.

The accident happened while the children were having their evening rice. When all the eating bowls were emptied, they begged Halmoni to come out to see the fine *miryek* they had completed.

But Dog had been there before her. Perhaps he thought there was a rat inside the snow man, or perhaps he had been chasing the black cat again. However it was, there were the prints of his scratching feet at the base of the snow man. And now instead of standing up tall and proud, the snow *miryek* had toppled far over to one side, and his hat had tumbled off. It was too late to rebuild their snow man that evening. It was to make the boys forget their disappointment that the Korean grandmother told them the story of the mole and the *miryek*.

"This is the story of a mole who lived down under the ground and a proud *miryek* who raised his head high to the heavens," Halmoni began. "All fathers and mothers think their children are perfect. Even the porcupine says its little ones are pleasant and smooth to the touch. But this Mole had a daughter who was truly a dragon child. Her skin was like softest satin, and her little nose and her claws were delicately pointed. Truly she was a perfect mole.

" 'Where shall we ever find a husband good enough for our dear daughter?' the mole asked his wife. 'She deserves the highest personage in all this universe.'

" 'We could send the go-between to the King of all the moles,' the mole mother replied. 'Nowhere in his kingdom would he find a bride so fair as our beautiful daughter.'

" 'But the King of the Moles is not the highest personage in the universe,' the mole father cried. 'None but the greatest is good enough for our jade daughter. The sky looks down on the Mole King. I shall go to the sky.'

" 'But I am not the all-highest,' the sky said when the mole came to his gate. 'The sun rules over me. The sun tells me when I am to be bright and when I am to be dark. Go find the sun, if you seek the all-highest.'

" 'Nor am I all-powerful,' the sun said to the mole. 'It is the cloud which tells me when my face shall be bright, and when my face shall be darkened. Go find the cloud.'

"So the mole knocked at the gate of the Cloud King. There he received this reply. 'It is true I cover the sun. I send forth the lightning. In my hands I hold the thunder. But I am not the all-highest. Go find the wind. The wind drives us clouds hither and yon across the broad sky.'

"When the mole stood before the wind, he trembled. Now he was sure he had found the greatest personage in all the universe. 'I seek the one who has power over all things,' he said, bowing low to the wind. 'My daughter is so perfect that only that one is fit to be her husband.'

" 'I am surely not that one, honorable Mole,' the wind said, blowing forth his great puffing breath. 'It is true I drive the clouds and the rain where I will. I can bend trees down to the ground. But there is one thing over which I have no power. That is the stone *miryek* that stands just above your underground home. I can puff and I can blow, but I cannot move that stone man even the breadth of a fly's wing.'

"Now this was indeed a surprise to the ambitious Mole. But he went back home again and bowed before the stone giant that towered so high above his underground home.

" '*Yé*, honorable neighbor,' the *miryek* said when the mole had told him of his quest. 'It is true I am strong. The sky cannot harm me, for all it looks down upon me. The sun cannot melt me, no matter how fiercely it burns. The clouds, with their rain, their lightning and their thunder, can in no way bring me misfortune. In all the broad universe there is but one person I fear.'

" 'Tell me who that one is, great *miryek*,' begged the mole.

" 'It is a mole!'

" 'A mole? How could that be, great one? A mole is but a small creature, living deep in the ground.'

" 'But it is only a mole who can dig the earth from under my feet. Should a mole dig there long enough, I would begin to topple over. Should he keep on digging, in time I would be lying face down on the earth. *Yé*, the mole is the one being I fear.'

"Now at last the mole was satisfied that he had discovered the husband best suited to his dragon child. He called in the go-between, and they soon arranged a marriage with a fine, handsome young mole. I am sure that they chose wisely, that the young couple lived happily together, and that they had many sons in their underground home."

"And I hope that the moles do not dig under the two stone *miryeks* the way Dog dug under our snow man," Ok Cha finished the story for her grandmother in her own gentle way.

THE

KING'S

SEVENTH

DAUGHTER

A S SOON as Old Pak the Gatekeeper brought the bad news, the Korean grandmother called all the children into the house.

"The Great Spirit of Smallpox is a guest in the courts of our neighbors next door. You must all stay indoors until he is gone. Everyone must speak softly, lest the Guest should be curious and fly over our wall. Not until he rides away again, shall wood be cut in our courts, nor shall nails be driven."

"Why, Halmoni? Why are we not to cut wood? Why are we not to drive nails?" Yong Tu asked.

"It is your own playmate Ho Cha who is now under the spell of that dreadful Guest. Do you want him to be marked with great pits in his face? Do you want our nails to blind his eyes? Don't ask such foolish questions."

The children well understood why their grandmother was so easily upset on this day. The coming of the Great Spirit of Smallpox to their neighborhood was a terrible thing. No charm was known that would drive him away before the full thirteen days of his visit were over.

Halmoni, like other Korean grandmothers, knew good charms against many of the spirits of sickness. When Ok Cha had pains in her stomach, her grandmother was wise enough to rub her well with a cat's skin. This, of course, frightened away the mice that were gnawing at her inside. When Yong Tu had whooping cough, which Koreans called the "donkey cough," Halmoni had sent at once for the medicine made out of donkey hair. It would help greatly, she thought, to dislodge the bad spirit that tickled his throat.

But Halmoni had no charm against this unwelcome Smallpox Guest. Nor had the wise doctors. Their long needles, thrust into a sick person's body, drove some spirits out, but not the Smallpox Fiend.

The *mudangs*, the women sorcerers, who came with their drums and their dancing, were the most powerful of all Korean doctors of those times. But even they could not shorten the stay of the Smallpox Guest.

"Thirteen days is a long time to be shut inside the house, Halmoni," the children complained.

Each morning the children peeped out at the neighbor's grass roof, hoping to see there the little wood horse on which the Smallpox Fiend would ride away. There would be on its back a wee bag of rice, some cash for his journey, and a bright red umbrella to shield him from the weather. It was well to be very polite to this curious guest. Whether he left joy or sorrow behind him depended on his good humor.

Ok Cha longed for the seesaw out in the pleasant court. Yong Tu missed his good games. He was just learning to kick the shuttlecock with the side of his foot, and he did not want to forget how.

On the twelfth day the Kims could hear the drums beating and the *mudangs* singing to honor the Smallpox Guest at its farewell feast. One of these wise women who knew so much about magic was always called in on such an important occasion.

"Ever since the King's Seventh Daughter cured the Queen of her sickness, the *mudangs* have been honored here in our land," the Korean grandmother told the children as they listened to the strange sounds that came drifting over their wall.

"That was in the days when there was more than one kingdom, and more than one king, in our Dragon Backed Country. One of these kings had six babies born to him, but, *ai*, all were girls. Six times had the fringe of straw, telling of a baby's birth, been hung across the palace gate. But not once had there been bits of charcoal knotted in it to proclaim the great joy that comes with the birth of a son.

" 'Do not feel sad,' the courtiers said to the King. 'Next time surely it will be a boy.' But the seventh child proved also to be only a girl. The King was so angry that he said, 'I will not have her! Cast her into the sea!'

"The Queen wept bitter tears. She loved all her babies, though they were but girls. But a wife must always obey her husband's command. That poor baby girl was locked up within a stone chest. The chest was taken in a boat far out on the sea. There it was dropped into the deep, deep, deep water.

"You will scarcely believe it, my children, but that heavy stone chest rode on the flashing blue waves, just like a boat. And at last it was washed up on the shore at the feet of a good priest. 'Here is the royal seal,' the priest said. 'This chest surely contains a prize of great value.' He opened the stone box with care. Behold, there was the baby, breathing and smiling as happily as if she had been in her dear mother's arms.

"Well, this priest knew the story of the King's Seventh Daughter. He feared that her angry father might harm the poor child if it were known she had been saved. So he hid her in the temple. He fed her and clothed her and made her days happy.

" 'Who am I, Holy One?' the princess asked her protector when she was old enough to wonder about her mother and father.

" 'You are a daughter of the forest, my little one,' the kind priest replied. 'Your father was the Spirit of the Bamboo, and your mother dwelt in the Odong Tree.' So the girl always made her bows to the bamboo and the odong, just as though they were human.

"As the years went by, the King's seventh daughter grew up safe and sound there in the temple. She did not learn the truth about her royal birth until one day a *mudang* came to seek out the priest.

" 'The good Queen is ill,' this *mudang* said. 'She is very ill. And she will die unless her lost daughter is found. I believe you can help me bring her to the Queen's chamber.'

"How that *mudang* knew where the girl had been hidden,

Yong Tu missed his good games out in the courtyard. He was just learning to kick the shuttlecock with the side of his foot.

I cannot say, but then those spirit doctors know most of the secrets of the universe.

" 'The King will be angry that his command to kill his seventh daughter was not obeyed. She will be in great danger,' the good priest objected.

" 'Neither the girl nor her protector need have any fears,' the *mudang* declared. 'It is the King himself who seeks the lost one to save his wife's life.'

"Indeed, there was only rejoicing when the King's seventh daughter appeared at the court. And the Queen did not die. But neither did she grow strong and well.

" 'There is a certain medicine in faraway India,' the *mudang* said to the King. 'Only one of the Queen's daughters can get it for her, and only when that has been done, will the evil spirits depart at last from her royal body.'

"Now India lies far beyond the broad plains and the high mountains of China. There were ten thousand chances against a traveler's safely going there and safely returning. The six older daughters all flatly refused to attempt the perilous journey. But the good seventh daughter, who had been reared by the priest, consented to go.

"Over the broad plains, across the deep rivers, and beyond the high mountains she traveled to seek the good medicine for her mother. Then over the high mountains, across the deep rivers, and across the broad plains she journeyed back again. Two long years it took her, but at last the medicine was brought and the good Queen was cured.

" 'How wise was the *mudang!*' all the courtiers cried. 'Had she not found the King's seventh daughter for us, our good Queen would have died.'

" 'How good is the King's seventh daughter!' the *mudangs* said among themselves. 'Had she not taken her long and dangerous journey to bring back the medicine, our cure would not have worked.' That is why the *mudangs* made the King's seventh daughter their own guardian spirit. Even today, my treasures, they call on her name in their songs that drive out the demons."

"But Halmoni," Ok Cha asked, "how could the King's seventh daughter ever have believed that her father was a bamboo and her mother an odong tree?"

"Why should her parents not have been spirits, Jade Child? And why not spirits that lived in the bamboo and the odong tree? Even today when a man mourns his dead father, he always carries a staff made of bamboo. When it is his mother who has ridden the dragon to the Distant Shore, he uses a staff made of odong wood. These customs our men follow may well have come down to us from this very same tale of the King's seventh daughter."

THE
WOODCUTTER
AND THE
OLD MEN
OF THE
MOUNTAIN

ONE summer evening after the eating tables had been carried away, Yong Tu sat on his grandmother's veranda with downcast face.

"What troubles my young *paksa?*" Halmoni asked kindly.

"I have been foolish, Halmoni," the boy replied. "I did not study today the pages of wisdom my father had set for me. Now he will not take me with him tomorrow when he goes to the country to look at the rice fields."

"And where were you, Dragon Head, when you should have been repeating wise words in the Hall of Perfect Learning?"

"The men in the Outer Court were playing a good game of *changki,*" the boy said, his eyes brightening. He still remembered how interested he had been in watching this popular Korean game of chess.

"*Yé,* that's how it always is." Halmoni nodded her head. "While the old men play *changki,* the ax handle rots."

"What does that saying mean, Halmoni?" Yong Tu

looked up, forgetting for the moment his disappointment about tomorrow's lost pleasure.

"*Ai*, blessed boy, the evening dark comes, but perhaps there is time for that story before you spread out your sleeping mat.

"The tale is about a woodcutter who might well have been called Min. He lived in the days before the trees on the mountain sides all were cut down. It would have been pleasant indeed under the grass roof of Min's little house, had it not been that his wife had such a bad temper. All the day long she scolded him. Even above the rat-a-tat-tat of her ironing sticks, her fretful voice could be heard.

"Who can blame that woodcutter for being glad to get away from such a shrew of a wife? He often sang as he trudged up the wooded mountain side beyond his village. His jiggy was easier far on his back than the blows his wife gave him with her ironing sticks.

"Like everyone else, Min often made a poem to honor the pleasures of a walk in the country. On this day he loudly sang this foolish song:

> '*Ho, the strong jiggy*
> *Rests light on my back.*
> *Of branches and twigs,*
> *For my stove there's no lack.*

> '*I'll pile them on high,*
> *Then pile on some more,*
> *Until I've enough*
> *To still my she-tiger's roar.*'

"There on that mountain side it was as quiet and peaceful as inside a temple. And because the sun was so bright and the sky was so blue, Min climbed higher and higher. He stopped now and then to bathe his face in the crystal water of a stream or to admire the wild flowers that grew amid the rocks.

"Then he came upon a little clearing hidden among the trees, just the place for him to rest after his climb. But there were those there before him. In the shade of a tree sat four curiously dressed old men. On a flat stone between them they were playing a game of *changki*. No doubt they played it in just the same way, Yong Tu, as the men you watched in the Outer Court this morning.

"With a polite cough of warning Min drew near the players. The old men looked up from their game and gave the newcomer greeting.

" 'Our visitor looks tired. No doubt he is thirsty,' the oldest one said. 'Give him a bowl of *sool*, boy,' he commanded the young servant who squatted near by. Min sat down beside the Ancient Ones, drinking the good wine and watching their game.

"The Old, Old Ones played slowly. They studied each move, and their wrinkled old hands crept back and forth over their chessmen, like snails on the ground. In the soft warm air Min grew drowsy. As he watched the game, his head nodded. Perhaps he even slept, for his head would lift with a jerk, when a player cried, *'Chang,'* as he made a checkmate.

"At last Min opened his eyes to see that the sun was low in the sky. 'The she-tiger in my house will be angry if I tarry here longer,' he said to himself, and he started to rise up from the ground. What could have happened to him? His joints were aching and stiff. He could scarcely get onto his feet. And when he looked down at his clothes, he found they were ragged and tattered. What was this white hair that fell from his chin? His beard and his hair were as snowy as those of the four ancient *changki* players. And where were they now? There was no sight nor sound of them.

" 'Those Old Ones must have been Mountain Spirits,' Min cried aloud. 'They have put their spell on me. They have taken away my good clothes and left me only these rags. They have stolen my ax. In its place they have put this crumbling stick of old wood and this rusty bit of iron. Even my jiggy frame has turned into dust, eaten up by the worms. *Ai-go! Ai-go!*' Min wailed. 'What will my wife say?'

"With tottering steps the poor woodcutter made his way down the mountain. As he drew near his village, his wonder grew even greater.

" 'The village did not look like this when I went up the hillside this morning,' he said to himself. 'No such house as this one stood out here on the edge of the rice fields. My old friend Cho had no new grass roof on his house. Who are all these new people gathered about the foodseller's shop?'

"There was even a strange dog in the gate hole of Min's own courtyard. 'Whom do you seek, Old Man?' asked a passing youth, who forgot his politeness at the sight of the woodcutter's tatters and rags.

" 'I seek the house of Min, the woodcutter. Is this not it?'

" '*Yé*, this was the house of Min, but he has been dead these thirty years. His son lives here now, but he is out on the rice fields.'

" 'And where is Min, the woodcutter?' the poor fellow asked.

" 'That was a sad thing, Grandfather,' the boy replied. 'It happened long before I was born, but they say he went out on the mountain to get brushwood, and he never came back. Perhaps a tiger ate him up. Or perhaps the spirits carried him off for cutting wood from a grave site.'

" 'But I myself am Min, the woodcutter, and this is my house,' the old man cried to the crowd that had gathered about. The people looked at one another in amazement and fright.

" 'Does a man ever return from the Distant Shore? Does he come out of his grave mound to live again?' they shouted. They began to curse Min. They shook their fists in his face. Then they ran away.

"Tears rolled down the wrinkled cheeks of the old woodcutter, for old he now was, as old as the ancient men of the mountain who had played *changki* under the tree in the glen.

"Just then there came toward the gate a very old woman. Her hair, too, was white. Her face had ten thousand wrinkles. And she carried a pair of ironing sticks in her hand.

" 'Can you tell me where I can find the wife of Min, the woodcutter?' the bewildered man asked politely. He was afraid to say again that he was Min. This old woman, too, might curse him for a demon. But the old woman only stared at him for a moment. Then she began to berate him.

" 'I know you well, Old Man, even after these thirty years. You are Min, himself, and I am your wife. How could you leave me all this time to work my hands to the bone to feed our young son? You worthless fellow, I'll teach you to go away like that again.' She seized the old man by his white topknot and began to belabor him on the shoulders with the ironing sticks.

" '*Hué*, this is good!' Min said, dodging her blows. 'Now indeed I am home again. Here is at least one who has neither changed nor forgotten me.'

"That, Dragon Head, is the story, from which we get the wise saying, 'While the old men play *changki*, the ax handle rots.' What does the saying mean? It means that if a boy spends too much time upon games, he does not get his lessons learned. Then he does not go on the good journey with his father tomorrow."

THE

GOOD

BROTHER'S

REWARD

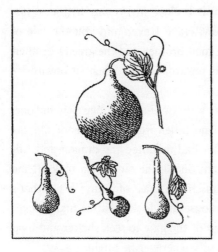

A NOTHER family had come to join the throng which crowded the houses inside the Kim courts. Another brother of the Master had fallen into bad luck and had brought his wife and his many children to seek the shelter of these tiled roofs.

"Why do they come to live with us, Halmoni?" Yong Tu asked his grandmother. "Why didn't they stay in their own house?" The boy was not sure he liked having his cousins there. They wanted to spin his tops and fly his kites. They were so many that Ok Cha seldom had a turn now on the swing in the Inner Court.

"Bad luck sought them out, blessed boy," the old woman explained. "Where should they come but to their wealthy brother? And how should he do otherwise than make them welcome? Our gates are always open to receive guests. Even a stranger is here offered a table of food. How then should a brother be turned away?

"And if this custom is broken, my young dragon, disaster surely would follow. Have I ever told you the tale of the two brothers, the good brother and the greedy brother, and how each one was rewarded? No? Then sit down here beside me, and listen well.

"Once long ago there were two brothers, one rich and one, like your uncle, who had fallen into the hands of misfortune. When their father had mounted the dragon and ridden away to the Distant Shore, the oldest son took all the family wealth for himself. Instead of filling his father's place as head of the house and looking after his younger brother, he put him out of the gate to seek shelter and food and clothes for his family wherever he might.

"To give these brothers names, we might call the elder greedy one Koh Sang Chip. The younger one might well have been named Koh Sang Hun. In the fine Koh family houses, Sang Chip lived alone with only his wife. No children had been sent to bless his selfish days. Sang Hun, on the other hand, dwelt with his wife and several sons in a little mud hut. Its ancient grass roof had such great holes in it that the rain fell through upon that family as if direct from the sky. At night those poor young people slept upon their tattered straw mats on a cold earthen floor. It was only by lying, huddled together, that they could keep warm.

"By weaving straw shoes and by doing whatever jobs he could find, Sang Hun barely managed to keep his little family alive. But often and often his children cried out for food. Even the rats complained to their neighbors that there was not one grain of rice in that house for the stealing.

" 'Send our youngest son to ask help from your rich brother,' Sang Hun's wife said one day to her unhappy husband. 'Surely when he sees that small boy's hungry look, he will give us a little from his great store of food.'

"But that greedy rich brother turned the boy away from his gate. 'I have food enough only for my own household,' he said roughly. 'My rice and my bean flour both are locked up tight in the storehouse. My bran I shall keep for my own cows. What extra grain there might be must go to my chickens. If I give you scraps from our table, my dogs will be angry. Go before they attack you!'

"When the little boy returned home, he was ashamed to repeat the cruel words his uncle had spoken. He only said, 'I have brought nothing. My uncle was not at home!'

" 'Well,' said his mother, 'I will sell these shoes off my feet. Their straw soles are still good. They will bring enough cash for a little rice for our supper.'

"But that night luck found its way to the good brother again. Sang Hun brought home a rich treasure from his day of gathering wood out on the mountain side. This treasure was a root of the medicine plant called *insam* (ginseng). Even the King and the Queen drank *insam* soup in the spring. The medicine sellers paid Sang Hun much money for the *insam* root. His wife's shoes could now be bought back. Together with her husband she could again go forth to seek work.

"Sang Hun's wife found a place among women winnowing rice, and the man acted as a porter with his wooden jiggy frame on his back, carrying loads for the rich folk of the village. And so they got through the winter.

"Spring came, and the swallows flew back from the south

to build their nests under the straw eaves of Sang Hun's little house. Soon there were baby birds in those nests. One day while Sang Hun was weaving sandals out in his courtyard, he saw a great roof snake glide out from the straw eaves towards the little birds. Before the man could drive the snake away, it had gobbled up all but one of the young swallows. That one had fallen out of the nest and struck the hard ground. When the man picked it up, he saw that one of its wee legs was badly broken.

"Gently big-hearted Sang Hun bound up the swallow's leg with splints made of dried fishskin. The children fed the bird and nursed it until it could hop about once again. Its wee leg was crooked, but it seemed strong enough and it began to fly about, chirping with joy.

"When the days began to grow short and the autumn nights began to grow chill, the little bird with the crooked leg hopped once more across Sang Hun's courtyard. It was chirping and chirping as if saying good-by before it flew off to the south.

"The next Spring the swallow with the crooked leg came again. It lit upon Sang Hun's hand, and into his palm it dropped a curious seed. On one side of the seed the man's name was written in golden brush strokes. On the other side were the words *Plant me! Water me!*

"This little bird with the crooked leg could not talk, but my grandmother always told me the seed was sent to Sang

Ok Cha seldom had a turn now on the swing in the Inner Court.

Hun by the King of the Birds. It was a reward for his kindness in saving the baby swallow from the roof snake and for healing its broken leg.

"Well, that seed sprouted and grew. Its plant climbed high up to the grass roof of that little house, and three enormous gourds hung upon its thick vine. About the middle of the Ninth Moon the man said to his wife, 'We shall cut the gourds down today. We can eat their soft pulp and we can make water bowls out of their hard shells.'

"When Sang Hun sawed the first gourd open, the couple saw a strange sight. Two menservants stepped out of it. They carried a fine table laden with silver bowls and bottles of wine. 'This bottle contains wine that gives men long life,' the spirit servants said to Sang Hun. 'This bottle has wine which makes the blind see. And this one will bring back speech to a dumb man.'

"The man and his family were silent with wonder as they sawed open the second gourd. At once their courtyard was filled with shining chests, with rich silks and rolls of shining grass linen. When the third gourd was opened, there came forth an army of carpenters with tools and strong pieces of excellent wood. Before the bewildered man's eyes there rose from his ground houses with tiled roofs, stables for horses, and storehouses for grain. Into his gates came a long train of bullocks, loaded with furniture, and with rice and other good food to fill his storage jars to the brim. Servants and horses and everything that a rich man's house holds came to Sang Hun out of these three magic gourds.

"Now news travels fast, and it was not long before Sang Hun's older brother heard of his good fortune. The greedy man came hurrying to find out how it had happened. When good Sang Hun told him the story of the swallow with the crooked leg, Sang Chip determined to try the same magic himself.

"With his cane he struck at every little bird he met during his journey home. Many he killed, but at last one little sparrow received a broken leg, and the cruel man caught it easily. He bound up the sparrow's leg with dried fish-skin splints. He kept it inside his house until the bird could hop again, just as Sang Hun had done. But there was no kindness in Sang Chip's cruel actions, and there was no twittering of thanks when that sparrow flew away from his courts. I have no doubt it twittered loudly enough when it told the King of the Birds about cruel Sang Chip who had broken its leg.

"When this sparrow with the crooked leg came back in the spring, it brought a seed for this brother, too. Greedy Sang Chip watched with delight when the green vine from it began to climb the side of his house. But the plant grew far too fast. It grew and it grew, until it smothered his entire dwelling. Its great creeping vines pried loose his roof tiles. Rain poured in upon all his treasured possessions. It cost him a great sum to have his roof made tight once again.

"Instead of three gourds there were twelve on his plant, giant balls almost as big as a huge *kimchee* jar. When the Ninth Moon came around, Sang Chip had to pay a carpenter several hundred strings of cash to open these gourds.

"Here were troubles indeed. Out of the first gourd stepped a troupe of traveling ropedancers. It cost Sang Chip much rice and many hundred strings of cash before those traveling dancers would go away from his courts. Even more money was needed to get rid of the procession of priests who came out of the second gourd. They demanded ten thousand strings of cash for rebuilding their temple of Buddha.

"Each gourd, sawed in two, brought fresh demands on Sang Chip's cash chests. A funeral procession, whose mourners had to be paid! A band of *gesang,* those singing girls whose music and dancing and bright waving flags always cost men so much! Traveling acrobats! A clown who needed much money for a long journey! A horde of officials demanding their 'squeeze' out of his tax money! And a band of *mudang* women, who threatened to bring the spirits of sickness into the house instead of driving them out! All these pests came out of the gourds to take away this greedy man's money. Jugglers, blind fortune-tellers, and poets had to be paid, until but little was left. From the eleventh gourd there stepped forth a great giant who took his very last copper cash away from Sang Chip.

" 'At least we have the twelfth gourd,' Sang Chip's weeping wife cried. 'Surely we have been punished enough. Surely there will be food or something else good inside this last one.'

"But when the carpenter sawed the twelfth gourd in two, there rolled forth clouds of smoke and hot darting flames. These destroyed every house, every stable, and every storehouse inside the rich brother's walls. His money was gone. His houses were burned to the ground! Where could the selfish man go now to seek shelter?

" 'We must ask help from my brother, Sang Hun,' he said to his wife.

" 'But will he not turn us away from his gates, as you turned away his hungry child?' the woman asked.

" 'I do not think so,' Sang Chip replied. 'Sang Hun has a heart as wide as the sky. He follows the ways of our father, who always gave with a big hand.'

"Sang Chip was right. His good younger brother opened his gates for them and brought forth tables of food. And just as we give a home to your unlucky uncle, Sang Hun made a place for his greedy brother. That was as it should be, my dragon, for there was plenty of room in the fine houses with which the Bird King had rewarded him."

THE

PANSU

AND THE

STABLEBOY

I'VE LOST my kite string, Halmoni. My good reel is gone!
I left it here on the chest in your room. But it is not
there." Yong Tu was panting with excitement and
distress. The boy was searching everywhere for the reel
of precious silken kite string which his father had given
him the day before.

"Have you looked well in all the houses here in the Inner Court, dragon boy?" his grandmother asked. "The
tokgabis may have rolled your reel under a chest. Or someone may have borrowed it. If you cannot find it yourself,
you will perhaps have to consult the blind fortuneteller. He
is a true *pansu*, who knows all things. It was a *pansu* who
found the horse that was stolen from Sin, the stableboy, in the old story. Though he might well have found it
himself if he had had his wits about him."

"Where did Sin find the horse, Halmoni?" said the boy,
who no doubt hoped he might find his lost kite reel in some
such place.

"It is not a long tale. Listen and I'll tell you just how it
was. Sin, the stableboy, was sent on an important journey

to a distant town. He carried a present to his master's friend, who was soon to celebrate his sixty-first birthday there. The young man rode upon his master's fine horse, and all went well until, on the way home, he stopped for the night at a country inn.

"When Sin rose from his bed on the inn floor next morning, his master's fine horse was gone. In its place there was only a poor sorry nag, as old as the Old, Old Men of the mountains. Lame in one leg and blind in one eye it was. You can imagine that Sin was afraid to go back to his master with such a broken-down horse as that.

" 'I cannot understand how this should have happened to me,' Sin said to the innkeeper. 'On this very journey I hung on the spirit trees a strand of hair from my horse's tail and bits of red cloth from his bridle. I threw pebbles on the piles of stones that honor the spirits along the way, and I bowed to the road gods. But no doubt it was an unlucky time for me to travel. Only last night I saw an arrow star shoot over the sky. That should have warned me!'

"At the innkeeper's suggestion Sin set out a bowl of rice for the Spirit of the Stable where his horse had been sheltered. Bowing low over it, he cried, 'Spirit of the Stable, here is my offering. Take it and eat it! And be kind enough to show me how to find my lost horse!'

"But no light came to poor Sin. He next sought out a *mudang*. The sorceress cast spells. She danced and she sang in the courtyard of the inn. She beat on her drum, the waist of which was almost as thin as that of an ant. But no fine horse came galloping back into the court.

" 'I must seek a *pansu*!' Sin said to the innkeeper. 'Only one such, who can look into both past and future, can help me in this trouble.' And he sought out a blind fortuneteller and begged him to tell him where to find his lost horse.

"Like all fortunetellers, this *pansu* had several ways of discovering secrets. First, he shook his little tortoise box with its eight bamboo sticks inside it. And he called to the spirits that lived in these sticks, 'Good people,' he cried, 'be kind enough to shed your light on our darkness. Help this good young man find his horse!'

"When the little sticks were thrown out on the table, the *pansu* felt them all over with his clever fingers, to find out how they had fallen. It was the same with the three coins he shook out of his little box that was shaped like a frog. Then the *pansu* nodded his head wisely, and he said to the wide-eyed stableboy Sin, 'Go! Buy a big bag of salt! Set it down before the sad animal that thief left in place of your master's fine horse. Let the horse eat all the salt it will. But do not give it water to drink. When the dawn comes again, you must set the sorry nag free. It surely will lead you to your lost horse.'

"Sin obeyed the wise words of the blind *pansu*. Horses dearly love salt, my son, and this one ate almost all Sin poured out before it. The sun was just giving the sky its morning brightness when Sin mounted the sorry nag and let it go where it would. Off it trotted at once. Along the highway to Seoul and through the crowds on the streets it galloped straight as an arrow. Sin had to hold fast to the saddle to keep his seat on its back.

"The horse finally took Sin to a village on the other side of the city. There at a certain house the animal stopped. It pushed the gate open with its impatient nose. Making straight for the water trough, the horse began drinking with great noisy gulps. Sin's eyes, however, were not fixed on that thirsty nag, but instead on his master's fine horse which stood tied in one corner of the courtyard.

" 'This is *my* horse,' cried Sin the stableboy to the Master of the House. 'You shall give him up to me, or I will go to the judge.'

"Well, perhaps the Master of that House was ashamed at being found out. Or perhaps he did not want the judge to have him paddled for stealing a horse. Whatever he thought, he gave up the fine horse and Sin rode it home.

"When the stableboy told his tale in his own Outer Court, all the men nodded their heads in admiration of the wisdom of the *pansu*. All of them, that is, except the old gatekeeper. 'You should have thought of that scheme yourself, Sin. Every stableboy should know that people never water their horses except in their own courts. By giving salt to that nag, you made him very thirsty. Where should he have gone but back to his own drinking place? And where should you have found your master's lost horse but in the stable from which that sorry nag came?' "

"That's a good story, Halmoni," said Yong Tu, "but it does not help me find my reel of kite string."

"*Ai*, then I must become a *pansu* and help you find it myself," the Korean grandmother said smiling. "Do you not see Ok Cha and her cousins making bamboo dolls there on the veranda? What could be better to make hair for a doll than a bit of unraveled silk string? And you must not scold Ok Cha too much," she said quickly, as Yong Tu started off towards his sister. "She has borrowed only a little string. Be gentle and be generous, my son! And who knows but you'll be rewarded with some strong, new kite paper."

THE

SPARROWS

AND

THE FLIES

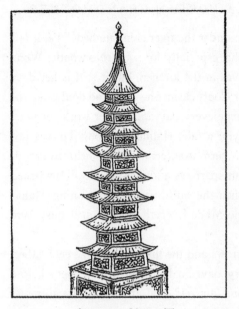

ONE afternoon Yong Tu and his sister found their grandmother lying down, under her tiger-skin rug. This seemed very strange, for at this time of the day she was usually busy with her embroidery needle.

"Are you sick, Halmoni?" Ok Cha and Yong Tu asked, speaking together, almost with one voice.

"*Ai*, precious ones, my head has been aching. Mice were running about inside it, but the good Spirit of this House answered my prayers and drove them away. Now I am only tired. Sit here beside me. Your talk will do me good."

"I will speak you a poem I made," Ok Cha cried. "It is not so beautiful as the ones Yong Tu makes, but still it is a poem. Wong Si says it is good. Listen, Halmoni.

> *"Why should we sweep*
> *Our court each day.*
> *When the South Wind*
> *Blows the dust away."*

237

The old woman under the tiger skin laughed. "*Yé*, it is a good poem, Ok Cha, especially for a girl. No wonder Wong Si liked it. She lives in the kitchen, but it still is her duty to sweep the Inner Court clean. She would no doubt like the South Wind to come every day and do her work for her."

"Now I'll tell you a tale, Halmoni." Yong Tu was impatient to take his turn at entertaining his beloved grandmother. "It's about sparrows and flies, and it all happened long, long ago, when the world was just beginning. Hananim, the God-Who-Made-Everything, was still busy here on the earth.

"Well, the sparrows and the flies did not like each other. They fought every day. So Hananim called them before him. 'What is your quarrel? You are a nuisance to man,' Hananim scolded them.

" 'The sparrows steal rice,' the flies said to Hananim. 'They go into the rice fields. They eat up the grain before the harvesters can gather it. They steal straw from the roofs of man's houses to build their nests. And they make such a noise that man cannot sleep. They are indeed a nuisance to man.'

" 'That is bad, very bad,' Hananim replied. 'The sparrows shall be punished.' And without giving the birds a chance to defend themselves, he had them paddled and paddled upon their poor little legs.

" '*Ai-go! Ai-go!*' those sparrows cried out, for the paddling hurt. They hopped up and down, up and down, on their poor little legs.

" 'Hear us too, Jade-Maker-of-Everything,' those unhappy birds cried. 'The flies are far worse than we are. They lay their eggs in the young rice. They spoil the good grain. They buzz about man's ears. They creep into his food. Who welcomes a fly in the early dawn when he wishes to sleep? *Ai*, the flies are even more of a nuisance to man than we are.'

"Well, the Jade Judge then ordered the flies also to have a good paddling. They stood before him rubbing their fore-feet together, just like any prisoner, rubbing his hands and begging that his punishment be made a little easier.

" 'I will pardon you both, if you will but cease your warfare,' Hananim said at last to the quarrelsome spar-rows and flies. 'But you must not forget and begin fight-ing again. Let the sparrows always hop instead of walk-ing like other birds! Then they will always remember the paddling they've had this day. Let the flies always rub their forefeet together whenever they come to rest. Thus they too will remember how they asked pardon here for their misdeeds.'

"There! Do you like that story, Halmoni?' Yong Tu asked anxiously as he ended his tale.

"It's a good story and a true one, no doubt," the Korean grandmother replied, "for the sparrows do hop and the flies do rub their forefeet together whenever they light. But that punishment has not done very much good. Spar-rows and flies are still nuisances to man. Sparrows still steal at harvesttime, and there's a fly on my nose at this very minute."

"I know a story about birds that were not nuisances," Ok Cha said eagerly. "Instead, they were helps. They saved a man's life. Shall I tell that story to you?"

"Tell it, little precious," the old woman replied smil-ing. The chatter of the children took her mind off the dull feeling that still remained in her head.

"My story is about a good Buddhist priest and some pigeons who made their nests under the eaves of his temple. The good priest fed the pigeons. He set water out for them. He allowed no one to harm them.

"When Spring came, there were eggs in the pigeons' nests under the temple eaves. And when the eggs hatched, there were baby birds. One day a great roof snake crept out from under the tiles and crawled towards the nest. Quickly before their enemy could reach the young birds, the priest struck the snake down. He killed it with a sharp blow of his walking staff."

"This sounds like the story Halmoni told us about the two brothers and Bird King," Yong Tu interrupted.

"It begins like it, Yong Tu, but it has a quite different ending," Ok Cha said patiently. "Listen! The next afternoon the good priest set out on a journey. With his wooden begging bowl in one hand and with a sturdy staff in the other, he went forth over the land to ask for cash and for rice from good-hearted people. When night came, he was already some distance away from the temple. There a farmer offered him shelter, and he went into his hut. The tired priest sat down in comfort upon the warm floor of the farmer's house, and his head nodded in sleep.

"Now one of the thankful doves from his own temple had followed the holy traveler to watch over him. While the man slept, the pigeon sat on a tree just outside the door. So it saw the great snake that crept towards the farmer's house. Somehow it knew that this was the Spirit of the roof snake the priest had killed. It had come to get even.

"'How shall I warn the good priest before that snake finds and kills him?' the pigeon thought. 'My voice is too faint. I must somehow sound the temple bell. That surely will waken him.'

"With flapping wings that pigeon flew back to the temple. With the help of its fellows, it tugged at the beam which the priests always swung against the sides of the bell. But their beaks were not strong enough. Then one of the pigeons flew with full force against the side of the bell. Boom! The sound of the metal, struck by the blow of the bird's dive, rang over the countryside. But the poor pigeon fell wounded onto the ground.

"Boom went the bell again, as a second pigeon sacrificed itself for its good friend, the priest. One after the other, the birds flew against the temple bell. The priest came running up the path to find out what the matter could be. He had waked just in time to escape the great Snake Spirit. When he saw the poor birds lying wounded on the ground, he knew they had rung the bell and saved his life."

"Do you think that priest could heal the wounds of the pigeons, Halmoni?" Yong Tu asked anxiously.

"Who knows, blessed boy?" The Korean grandmother spoke comfortingly. "There are many stories about animals whom the good Buddha saved during his life on earth. No doubt, his priest found some way to put splints on the broken bones of his little protectors, just as Sang Hun healed the leg of the swallow in the story, 'The Good Brother's Reward.' "

CLEVER

SIM

WHO

WOULD

"SQUEEZE"

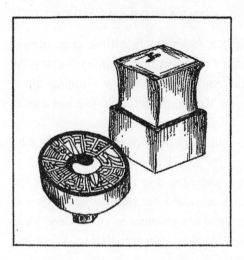

Yong Tu and Ok Cha were helping to polish one of the great wooden chests in the apartment of their grandmother. They were rubbing the carved pieces of brass which served as its hinges and ornaments. Under their soft cloths the brass shone like pure gold against the gleaming brown wood.

There were many such chests in the houses of the Kim household. There were clothes chests and treasure chests. There were huge cash chests like the one on which the two children were working. Smaller chests had drawers to hold rice powder for the women's faces, red color for their lips, and black oil for their hair.

Halmoni sat on her tiger-skin rug on the floor, putting the finishing stitches into a new coat collar for her very best silk jacket. Coat collars in Korea had to be replaced often because of the black oil stains which kept the women's hair neat.

"I can't reach the top bits of brass, Halmoni. This cash chest is so tall," Yong Tu complained.

"It takes a big box to hold only a little cash, blessed dragon. Big enough for a man to hide inside—that's the size of a cash chest. And it was while he was hiding in just such a chest, that the King's spy in the old tale had a great fright."

"You've never told us that story, Halmoni," Ok Cha said hopefully.

"Go on with your polishing, and I'll tell it now. It is the tale of clever Sim, who would not stop taking a 'squeeze' from the poor people of the province he ruled. Good kings and good ministers, like your own grandfather, do not like men who squeeze.

"There was such a good king once in this land, and such a good minister, too. It was the Minister—in truth, not a wise man—who appointed his cousin Sim to be governor of that province. Now Sim, this cousin, was clever, far too clever, as you will see.

"The Minister had a white horse without a dark hair on its hide. But he was not satisfied. He wanted a black horse, and it was Sim who provided it. Sim found a gray horse, and he painted it all over black. He brushed every hair with shining black varnish, so that the horse's coat shone like the sides of a black lacquer box. It was to reward Sim for the gift of this shining black horse that the Minister gave him a province to rule over.

" 'I shall invent many taxes,' this new Governor said to himself. 'I shall squeeze wherever I can. I shall grow very rich!' Squeeze Sim did, and grow rich he did, too. He had a fine house, and he had a splendid sedan chair, which eight men carried for him. He liked to ride also in his handsome chair on one wheel with four men to guide it as it rolled along over the city streets. It was a fine sight to see Sim come riding along in this one-wheeled chair. Sitting high on the seat, atop the little wheeled pedestal, he looked very proud. Ordinary men hurried to get out of his way. Travelers upon horseback dismounted to bow as he passed. They knew he must be a very important official indeed to ride on a monocycle.

"So much squeeze did Sim take, and so rich did he become, that word came to the King. 'Find out about this Governor Sim,' the King said to his ministers. 'Send Yun to that province to bring back the truth about the squeeze he is taking away from the poor people.'

"Now Sim had a friend in the King's court, who warned him of the coming of Yun, the first spy which the King sent. 'This Yun is an honest man,' so said Sim's informer. 'You cannot turn him away from the truth by offering him any part of your squeeze. But he is a timid man. He will come riding on a slow mare, with a sucking colt by her side.'

"Clever Sim easily thought of a way to make the King think that his spy, Yun, was crazy. Sim's men stole the mare's colt, and they fastened a tiger's skin on its back. Then they hid it along the roadway which Yun, the spy, had to travel. When the mare came along with Yun sitting lazily upon her back, Sim's men loosed the colt in the tiger's skin. The tiger's head covered the colt's face, and the tiger's tail, stiffened with a piece of bamboo, curved over its back.

"When the mare saw the colt coming towards her, she smelled only the tiger's skin. And she straightway turned tail and galloped back towards the Capital. Along the road, through the streets, and into the Palace court they fled.

Yun tried his best to keep his seat on the frightened mare, and the colt, looking for all the world like a tiger, bounded behind. Everyone fled in panic from this curious beast, until the colt began to take its milk from the mare's bag. The courtiers burst into loud laughter at the sight of a mare suckling a tiger. The King, thinking Yun had played this trick himself, exiled him to the lonely island which men call Quelpart.

" 'Send Sun this time. He is not so foolish as Yun,' the King next commanded. And soon Sim received warning of the coming of this second spy, who should report on his evil 'squeezing' to the King. 'This spy, Sun, is not timid. He rides a white mule, and there is no colt. But he dearly loves drinking wine and listening to singing girls.'

"So at every inn Sim stationed *gesangs*, the very best singing girls he could find in his province. They filled the spy's wine bowls again and again. They delayed him as long as they could with their merry songs and their graceful dances. It was when the spy was in the finest of all these inns that Sim played the best of all his tricks upon Sun.

"In that inn rich food was set out for the spy and the innkeeper's pretty wife herself gave him wine and entertained him. 'The only danger to you, Honorable Guest,' the young woman warned Sun, 'is my husband's homecoming. The master of this inn is a jealous man. When he comes and finds you still here with me, you will do well to hide.'

"So when there were sounds of the innkeeper's coming,

The mare smelled the tiger's skin and galloped away.

the spy gladly crawled into a great cash box, like the one you are polishing, Dragon Boy. The woman snapped the huge brass lock shut, pushing its great prongs firmly into their socket.

"The innkeeper also played his part well. He pretended to be angry, and the spy inside the box trembled when he heard his cross words. 'Where is that traveler?' the man scolded his wife. 'His white mule is outside. I know you have hidden him. I'll have you no longer as wife in my house.'

"'But how shall we divide all the things we own together,' the woman said, also pretending to be angry. They quarreled and quarreled, but they succeeded in dividing up everything, except the cash box. Each claimed that for his own. At last, to his horror, the prisoner inside it heard the man say, 'Well, we will have to saw the cash box in two.'

"'It is far too fine a chest for that,' the wife objected. 'We will take it to the judge.' The spy was relieved to have escaped death from a saw, but he was sure he would be paddled if the chest were opened up before the judge.

"'I cannot decide this question with fairness,' said Governor Sim, who played the part of the judge. 'But I'll give you two hundred strings of cash for it, and I'll keep it myself.' The innkeeper and his wife went away home, very well paid for their part in the play-acting.

"Sim loaded the cash box between carrying poles and sent it to the King. Speaking loudly so that the spy, Sun, should not fail to hear him, he said to the porters, 'Drop this chest in the river if you hear any noises that sound as though there are spirits inside!' You can believe the poor, frightened prisoner made no noise at all until that chest was set down at last before the King and his ministers.

"How the ministers laughed when the box was unlocked and poor Sun was dumped out! His legs were so cramped with his long ride in the cash box that he could only crawl about on all fours like a turtle.

" 'Here is another trick,' the angry King cried, and he sent the second spy, Sun, to Quelpart Island, too.

" 'Kun, the third spy, comes,' Sim's friend at court wrote him. 'He never drinks wine, and he prefers temple bells to *gesangs'* singing. He is not at all timid. He stands in awe only of the shaven-headed priests of the temple.'

"Clever Sim was not long in planning a way to trick this man, too. Like you and Ok Cha, Dragon Boy, Sim well knew the story of the woodcutter who watched the Mountain Spirits play *changki* and who took a nap that lasted for thirty years. For getting rid of Kun, the third spy, he chose that story to help him.

"When Kun arrived at the halfway inn, he heard sounds of strange temple music up on the hillside. 'It is the gods assembling on their sacred mountain,' the innkeeper told him, following Governor Sim's orders. 'They come here only once in a thousand years. Only very good people are allowed to visit them there.'

"The pious messenger, Kun, trembled with excitement. 'I go to the temple. I worship the Great Buddha. Perhaps the gods would receive me.'

"So Kun climbed the mountain, just as Sim had meant he should do. There in a dell he found four old men dressed in long flowing robes like those of the mountain gods on the screen in your father's Hall of Perfect Learning. There were four young boys, also in curious clothing, waiting upon the old men and handing round wine. Urged by the mountain gods, Kun drank from each bowl. The rich wine was strong, and he fell into sound sleep.

"Before he awoke, Sim's men dressed him in tattered clothing. They put a rotting stick in the place of his staff, and they carried him off far into the high mountains.

"Next morning when Kun came again to his senses, he thought at first he had been taken by the gods to Heaven itself. But he soon saw this was not so, and he started down the mountain again. As if by accident, a man gathering brushwood came up the path. 'Tell me, good sir,' poor Kun inquired of him. 'Have you heard what became of the King's messenger, Kun, who was yesterday at the inn?'

" 'There was such a one, I have been told,' the wood-cutter replied. 'But they say he was carried off by the gods two hundred years ago.'

" 'That heavenly wine must have put me to sleep,' the befuddled Kun said to himself. 'I have slept two hundred years. That is why my clothes are so tattered, why my staff has rotted away, why the King's seal is so rusted.'

"Shaking his head in dismay, he went back to the inn where he heard the same story. The innkeeper brought forth fresh clothes without any holes. He found him a chair and some bearers to carry him home. To Kun's surprise, his own family looked just as they had when he had started out on his journey. So also did the King and the King's Minister.

" 'You have not changed in all these two hundred years,' Kun exclaimed to the King. And when he insisted he had drunk with the gods, they declared he was crazy. Kun, too, was sent to join the other two spies on the faraway island of Quelpart in the south."

"And what became of Sim, the Clever Squeezer, Halmoni?" Yong Tu asked, giving a last polish to a brass bat with broad curving wings.

"The King gave up trying to stop him from squeezing. 'He is far too clever to be caught,' he said to the Minister. 'We had best bring him back here to the court. We can set him the task of calming those people who clamor for favors at our palace gate.'

"Well, Sim used his clever tricks to turn these pests one against another. They quarreled so amongst themselves that they forgot to complain of their wants to the King. Some say Sim was made the King's Treasurer, so that he could squeeze as much as he liked without causing distress to the poor."

THE

TIGER

HUNTER

AND

THE MIRROR

O K CHA was admiring herself in a shining mirror she had taken from the drawers of the treasure chest in her grandmother's room. The round disk of silver shone like the full moon, the little girl thought. She liked the graceful bamboo leaves carved on its back and the embroidered red silk that covered its short, flat handle.

"Whom are you bowing to, little precious?" the old woman said smiling. She was amused at the faces the child was making at her own image in the silver mirror.

"Who should it be but me, Halmoni?" Ok Cha replied, looking surprised at the question.

"I thought perhaps you were like Pil, the tiger hunter, who did not know at first the secret of the mirror which the King sent him."

"Why did the King send a mirror to a tiger hunter, Halmoni?"

"Why else but that Pil had killed a ferocious tiger that had brought terror to his whole kingdom. No ordinary beast was this striped gentleman from the mountains. White whiskers as long as your hand he had, and fur as thick and as soft as softest silk. But that tiger had also teeth as sharp as my needles, and jaws so huge they could carry off a grown man.

"There was a great to-do in Pil's court when the King's messengers came. Nothing so splendid as their fine feathered hats and their bright red-and-green robes had ever been seen there. In the great chest they carried were rich gifts to reward this hunter who had slain the terrible tiger. There were silks of many colors, green as the young rice plants, red as the red peppers, and blue as the sky. There were fans and a long pipe with a carved silver bowl and many other things, too. But, strangest of all, was a silver mirror like that you hold in your hand, blessed Jade Child.

"Now, for all he was such an experienced hunter, Pil was a simple man, and his family, like him, were all countryfolk. They knew almost nothing about the ways of a city. They never had seen such a shining white metal disk as the one Pil lifted out of the King's treasure chest.

"Pil's wife was the first to look closely at the clear surface of the silver mirror. Straightway the woman gave a loud cry. 'Ai-go! Ai-go!' she wailed when she saw there her own woman's face looking out. 'Here my husband has brought home a second wife to take my place. Or perhaps she's a singing girl. That is much worse. Whoever she is, I'll not have her in my house.' Of course never having owned a mirror before, this woman had never really seen her own face, except in the dull waters of the stream where she washed the family clothes.

"Pil came running to find out what such cries meant. He, too, peered intently into the mirror. Naturally, the face he saw there was that of a man. He, too, flew into a rage, screaming, 'What man is this? My wife has hidden a strange man in our Inner Court,' and he started towards the woman as if he would strangle her.

"The hubbub brought the tiger hunter's old mother hurrying to see what was the matter. When she looked into the magic silver disk, she saw, of course, a face covered with wrinkles and topped with gray hair. It was for all the world like that of her troublesome neighbor who was always borrowing food. 'Ai, here is that beggar from down the road,' she said under her breath. She could not understand why, when she turned around, she found nobody there.

"The grandfather, in his turn, thought the face he saw in the mirror was that of the old *pansu* who had come to demand payment for choosing a grave site. 'How did that *pansu* make his way into our house without somebody seeing him?' and 'Where has he gone now?' he cried, looking about him and running to look out of the door.

"The story of the strange object in the house of Pil, the tiger hunter, spread through the village. The neighbors gathered, and all tried to solve the problem in vain. There were many loud arguments as each one saw his own unfamiliar face in the mirror.

"Even the village judge could not understand the round silver disk. When he saw the head of a man, capped with his own judge's hat, staring out at him, he began to complain. 'Why is there another judge sent here from the Capital?' he scolded. 'Have I not filled my place well? Call out the tiger hunters! Let them drive this strange judge away from our peaceful village!'

"Happily, the messengers had not yet ridden back to the King's court. How they laughed when they learned of the commotion this royal gift of a mirror had caused!

" 'Ho! Ho! Ho!' they laughed. 'Ha! Ha! Ha! Ho! Ho! Ho! Honorable Judge,' they said to the village elder, 'it is yourself you see there in that mirror.' And they explained how the shining metal gave back the face of him who looked into it.

" 'Ho! Ho! Ho!' Pil laughed louder than anyone else at the joke on himself. 'Ha! Ha! Ha!' cried his wife, happy that she did not have any cause to be jealous of a second woman under her roof. 'Ho! Ho! Ho!' All the people of that village held their sides, whenever they looked into their own mirrors—for, of course, each household now had to have at least one such wonderful 'seeing glass.' And the tiger hunter Pil, himself, was the man they chose to ride on a fine horse to the King's city to buy them."

THE

ROOSTER

AND

THE

CENTIPEDE

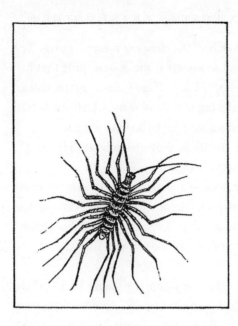

Pᴀɪɴᴛᴇᴅ in bright colors on a square tablet of wood, a fierce rooster hung on the edge of the veranda in the Inner Court.

"It drives the centipedes away," Halmoni often explained to the children. "But you must keep watch for them just the same," she always added.

Those long crawling creatures, with their many legs moving like the oars of a boat, were feared by everyone in the Inner Court. None in the Kim household would ever forget the time when Yong Tu picked one up in his hand, nor how nearly its poisonous bite came to sending him off to the Distant Shore.

"That centipede was twice as long as my hand," the boy told his friends. "My hand and my arm grew very fat. Only when the *mudang* made charms over me, did the pain go away."

Halmoni had watched the *mudang's* every move. The sorceress danced and screamed at the poison spirit that had entered the little boy's body. The Korean grandmother, however, thought the rag soaked in wine, which she herself put on the bite, had a good deal to do with the cure.

"Why does the centipede fear the rooster, Halmoni?" Ok Cha asked one afternoon.

"Because of the rooster's sharp beak, of course, child. Then, too, the rooster and the centipede have been enemies for ten thousand years. There are many tales about that."

"Could you remember one now?" the little girl asked eagerly.

"I can remember the one about the young man and the woman who once had been a centipede. That was a curious happening. It took place many hundreds of years ago, probably right here in our own city of Seoul.

"The man came of a family whose name was Chu. He was young and well-mannered, and he earned his rice by finding customers for an important silk merchant. So polite a manner had Chu that when he stood on the street and asked people to buy, many followed his beckoning into the silk shop.

" 'Buy silk! Fine silk! No better silk in all the land!' Chu was crying this one day when the maidservant of a rich widow walked by. Under his persuasion she bought of the best the silk shop afforded, and she paid for her purchase with shining gold coins out of her embroidered belt pocket.

"Not many days later, the maidservant came to the Street of Silk Merchants again. Though young men from other silk shops begged her to enter, she waited for Chu. And again she bought much. A third time, and a fourth time, she came to the silk shop. The silk merchant was pleased, and it meant good earnings for Chu.

"One afternoon the widow's maidservant politely requested Chu to accompany her home. Her mistress wished to talk with him about some special silk she wished to buy for a screen. Now this lady was a widow, and Chu himself was a widower, his young wife having died when the Spirit of Smallpox entered his courts. Both were young. Both were handsome. It is not strange that before long the widow and Chu were married, and the young man went to live with her in her rich home.

"All went well. Chu was happy. Never had he known so kind and so pleasant a woman as his new wife. He had fine coats of silk, and each meal was as bountiful as an Ancestors' Feast.

"When he walked abroad, Chu usually crossed the 'Chicken Bridge' near his home. One evening as he stepped upon it, he heard a voice calling his name. 'Chu, Chu, my son!' the voice said. 'Your father speaks. Your father warns you of danger. That person in your house, that woman, brings you bad luck. You must put her to death. Crush her as you would a centipede that crawls near your foot.'

" 'How should I kill my beautiful wife?' Chu replied to the voice that came from under the bridge. 'She is good. She is kind. She has brought me only good luck. I could never do her harm.' And he went on his way.

"The next time the young man crossed over the Chicken Bridge, the voice of his dead father came to him again. 'Kill that person in your house, my son. Your father's spirit commands you. She is a demon in woman's form. If she does not die before close of the fifteenth day, your own spirit will ride the winds to join me here on the Distant Shore.'

"Now the young man was troubled. The voice that gave him this dire command sounded just like that of his own father. He was a good son who always had obeyed the words of his parents. But when he thought of the comfort and kindness which he had got from his good wife, he knew he never would kill her.

"His heart was heavy. The fifteenth day dawned, and the hours passed one by one. At evening he went into the Inner Court. His wife did not move towards him as usual. She only sat on the soft white mat on the floor, as if lost in a dream.

"As Chu watched in silence, her face turned first to dead white, then to pale green. The woman began to groan and to shiver. The man was spellbound. He did not dare touch her or call out her name, for he could see she was bewitched. At last, however, the sickness passed away from his wife's face. Joy filled Chu's heart when her skin cleared. She opened her eyes, and she began to speak to him.

" 'Why did you not kill me, as the voice under the bridge commanded you, Master of my House?'

" 'What strange words do you speak? What is their meaning?' Chu replied to her. 'How did you know about the voice under the bridge?'

" 'I will tear the paper out of the windowpane of your understanding so that you may see clearly into the heart of that curious happening under the bridge,' Chu's wife said to him. 'It is a strange story, but it has a golden ending. By your kindness and your faithfulness you have released me from a terrible prison.

" 'You must know that, in an earlier life, the Jade Emperor of Heaven decided to punish me for some misdoing. He changed me from a woman into a centipede, and he set a great rooster to torment me. Through one life after another, that rooster has pursued me. Only after a thousand years had gone by, was I permitted to take on my former shape and become a woman again. But still my enemy followed me.

" 'Once I had become a woman, I was too large and too strong for the rooster to kill all by himself. His only hope was to persuade some man to perform the dreadful deed for him. It was the rooster's voice you heard, my husband, imitating your dead father. And it was your good heart that kept you from obeying that false command.

" 'This day ends the time that was given the rooster to destroy me. My spirit was fighting with his spirit when you came into the Inner Court this afternoon. As you see, I won the battle. Now, forever, am I free of him. Always and always, now, I may remain a woman and your wife. Peace lies before us.'

"Next morning when Chu came to the Chicken Bridge, he climbed down to the spot whence the strange voice had come. There on the ground he found an enormous white rooster. Old, very old, it was. And as tall as Yong Tu. The rooster was dead, quite dead, my children. Never again did Chu's wife have to fear him. But to this day, a rooster will attack a centipede whenever the two meet."

THE

ROCK

OF

THE

FALLING

FLOWER

W HY does our Jade Emperor let those 'little men' from Japan come into our land? No good will come of it." Halmoni shook her old head, and a frown darkened her calm face. Kim Hong Chip, her eldest son, had just returned from the Korean seaport of Fusan, and he had been telling his mother of the many Japanese he had seen there.

It was not hard to recognize the Japanese. They had the same narrow eyes as Koreans, and the same broad high cheekbones. But their olive-skinned faces were darker, and they were not nearly so tall.

Ever since the Emperor had signed the "paper of peace," permitting Japan to trade in the Hermit Kingdom, more and more of these "little men" came every year. Yong Tu's father even pointed them out to him as they walked together on the streets of Seoul. The boy looked at them, half curiously, half in fear. Halmoni had told the children about terrible things that had happened in the past when the Japanese armies crossed the sea to try to conquer their land. There were tales of people killed and cities burned.

Worst of all, Yong Tu thought, was the story about the thousands of pickled Korean noses and ears which the Japanese soldiers took home with them after one of their visits. In the Japanese city of Kyoto, Halmoni said, these Korean noses and ears were put in a tomb. There was even a tablet set up to boast about the cruel deed.

"A shrimp between whales is our Little Kingdom," the old woman declared again and again. "The great whale of China has often tried to swallow us up. But we made friends with China, and, like an elder brother, China helped us keep off the other whale called Japan. That island country of Japan has learned the strong magic of men from the Western Seas. It has grown very powerful. *Yé*, Japan wants to conquer the wide eastern world. It would make our little land a steppingstone to get at its giant enemy, China.

"*Ai-go! Ai-go!* Not always will our tortoise ships turn back the Japanese fleet." The Korean grandmother spoke firmly, shaking her old head up and down.

The story of Admiral Yi and his ironclad ship, shaped like a tortoise, was one of Yong Tu's favorite war stories. And it was a true story.

"Nearly three hundred years before you were born, Yong Tu," Halmoni used to say to the boy, "the Japanese Navy set sail once again. Its ships were ferrying many thousands of soldiers across the sea to attack us. But this time a surprise was awaiting those ships. Coming to meet them from our Korean shore was a vessel whose like they never had seen. Shaped like a giant tortoise it was, with flame spurting forth from its sharp dragon's head. Flames burst from its sides also, from gun openings cut just above the holes for the oars.

"Strangest of all, its curved tortoise back was covered with thick plates of strong iron. The shots from the Japanese guns bounced off this armor, falling harmlessly down into the water. None could destroy this ironclad tortoise ship. The Japanese soldiers and sailors were sure it was a spirit ship.

"But the flaming shots from the tortoise ship which dropped on their decks quickly set the wooden Japanese war vessels afire. Its sharp dragon's head rammed holes in their sides. Soon all were destroyed. And the signal fires on the mountains told the King that our enemy had been driven away once again."

Halmoni was telling her grandson about the very first iron-clad ship ever invented. The name of its maker, the clever Korean admiral, Yi Sun Sin, was honored throughout the entire Kingdom. It seems strange that more of these tortoise warships were not built, but the peaceful people of this Land of Morning Calm were content with their victory. "We can always build more tortoise ships when the need comes," they said, for they thought they had so frightened the Japanese that they would never attack them again.

Ok Cha's favorite war story also told of a victory over the Japanese. In this story a young Korean, Nonga, the singing girl, danced a cruel Japanese general into the deep river and helped save her country.

"But that happened before the coming of the tortoise

ship, blessed girl," Halmoni explained. "It was when a great battle was being fought on the land. The dwarf men from Japan had come with ten thousand times ten thousand soldiers. They carried battle axes and long swords, daggers and spears, and they roamed over our country, killing our people and destroying our homes.

"*Ai*, that was a bad time. Our tiger hunters and our other soldiers made a brave fight, but they were not strong enough. There was no general in all Korea so fierce as that one who led the Japanese Army. 'If we could only kill the General, our luck would turn,' the word went through the land.

"As if he were a fierce Mountain Uncle, the tiger hunters set traps for the Japanese General. But he was too wary. The *mudangs* made their loudest charms, and the *pansus* chose lucky days for our attacks. But not one was successful.

"The Japanese General and his officers at last had conquered the whole country, ending with the little city of Chinjoo to the west. In spite of its double walls, they entered the town. They killed the Korean general who had defended Chinjoo, and they cut off the heads of the judge and the other city officials. The soldiers and tiger hunters scattered and fled, hiding themselves high up in the hills.

" 'Now we can rest,' the Japanese General said to his officers. 'What better place is there to celebrate victory than

Ok Cha's favorite war story was about Nonga, the singing girl who danced the Japanese General into the deep river.

here in this pleasant valley?' Chinjoo was built on the banks of a fair, sparkling stream, where the water deepened and widened to form a true river. From the rocks along the river bank there could be seen many fine fish swimming about in the crystal clear waters. And it was the resthouse on that river which the Japanese General chose for his merrymaking.

"*Hué*, there was noise in that place when those 'dwarf men' celebrated their victory over our land. There was drinking and singing. There was laughing and shouting.

"When the merriment was at its greatest, a girl dressed in the garb of a *gesang* appeared at the door of the resthouse. She was as fair as a silver moon in a starlit sky. Never had that Japanese General seen one to compare with her for beauty and grace.

" 'How is it you are here?' the General said to the singing girl. 'How dare you brave the enemies of your country like this? All your men are away, hid in the hills. There is none to defend you.'

" 'I have come to thank the Great General for killing the judge of this city of Chinjoo,' the singing girl said. 'I am called Nonga, the *gesang*. My father was a good man, but a neighbor wrongly accused him before the judge. The cruel judge ordered that my poor father be paddled, and they beat him and beat him until they beat him to death. I vowed then that I would reward any man who should help me take revenge on that judge. You have cut off his head, and I have come here to keep my vow. I shall dance for you my best dances and sing for you my sweetest songs.'

"The General gave the fair Nonga a seat at his side. He ordered tables of food and bowls of wine brought. Nonga's singing delighted him, and he wished her also to dance. 'There is a flat rock down there on the river bank,' the *gesang* said to the General. 'The air is cool and fresh, and one can look far, far down the green valley. Let us go to the river bank. There I will dance for the Honorable General.'

"The beauty and grace of the *gesang* seemed to have bewitched the Japanese General. He followed her down to the water's edge and across the curious rocks which lay along the river bank. The girl led the way to a great table rock that rose high, high out of the water into the air. And she seated the General upon it, giving him more and more wine to drink from the bottles she had brought along in her basket.

"Then Nonga began to dance. Her full, gay-colored sleeves floated in the soft air, and her graceful posing was like that of a flower bending in the summer breeze. The General nodded his befuddled head in time to her singing. Then he rose up to dance with her.

"This was what Nonga had plotted and waited for. Winding her arms round the General's waist, she danced with him nearer and nearer the edge of the cliff. Then with one mighty leap she jumped off into the deep water, taking her country's enemy with her.

"The Japanese soldiers on the bank of the river saw the hands of the General reaching out of the water toward the rock. But they saw, too, that the arms of the brave singing girl held his waist fast. As they watched, she dragged him down with her to the watery kingdom of the River Dragon."

"What happened then, Halmoni?" Ok Cha could scarcely wait for the happy ending of the story.

"Why, I suppose the River Dragon rewarded the good

singing girl, Nonga, for her courage and her self-sacrifice. Perhaps the Dragon himself ferried her to the Heavenly Shore. Or perhaps he sent her back to earth again to marry a prince, like the girl in the story of Sim Chung, the blind man's dutiful daughter.

"But the death of that Japanese General was indeed the turning point of that war. When they heard the news, the scattered Korean soldiers gathered once more. The tiger hunters returned from the hills. Then the signal fires on the mountains told the King that his land was saved once again from the dwarf men from Japan.

"In Chinjoo a shrine was set up to honor Nonga, the *gesang*. People say once a year, on the date of her death, the water of that little river turns as red as blood in memory of her noble death. Some call this place the 'Righteous Rock,' but my grandmother always spoke of it as the 'Rock of the Falling Flower.'"

EPILOGUE

—MANY,

MANY YEARS

LATER

OK CHA'S

STRANGEST

STORIES

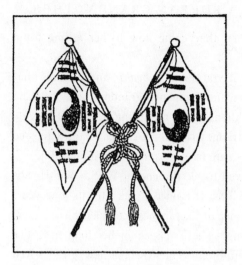

M Y GRANDMOTHER always said no good would come
of letting the Japanese into our land. And she spoke
wise words." Ok Cha said this to her own grandchildren again and again in her old age. Many, many years
had passed since she was a little girl, playing in the calm
Inner Court of the Kim household. When she was fifteen
years old, she had been put into the emerald-green dress of
a Korean bride. With richly packed, brassbound chests
going before, she journeyed in the gaily decked bride's
chair to the Inner Court of her husband's family. Here her
children and her grandchildren had been born. Here she
hoped to live until the end of her life.

Few remembered that her girlhood name had been Ok
Cha. Now she was "Halmoni" to all the children in the
household. It was about her that they gathered when they
came home from school. Her face was even more wrinkled
than that of her own grandmother had been. She, too,
loved her grandchildren, and her bright eyes beamed

with pleasure when they came now to her asking for a story.

"The tales I tell you about *tokgabis* and animals that could talk came to me from my grandmother," Ok Cha often told the children. "They are strange tales, but they do not seem half so strange to me as the things I have witnessed with my own eyes here in our Land of Morning Calm."

Ok Cha had lived to see the end of World War II. She had lived to see Korea free once again after its long years of being the prisoner of its Japanese conqueror.

And what changes she had seen in her long life! The children of her family all went to school now, girls as well as boys. Swinging their brass rice bowls in little string bags, they started off gaily each morning. The lessons they learned were very different from those which her brother, Yong Tu, used to repeat in his grandmother's apartment. In addition to the wise sayings of the ancient Chinese teachers, they studied geography, history, science, and arithmetic, just like the children of Western lands.

These modern young Koreans knew all about streetcars, airplanes, and radios. They had ridden in busses and automobiles and even in trains, which some old people still called "fire wagons." It amused these children greatly to hear their old grandmother tell of the early times when such things were first brought into their country.

"Open the door to one stranger, and a hundred rush in," Ok Cha often said, going back in her memory to the days when Korean ports were first opened to foreign trading ships. "I well remember my first sight of a man from America. I was riding with my mother in our sedan chair, and I was peeping out through the curtains. *Ai,* I was frightened by his sickly white face, his fuzzy hair, and his pale eyes.

"Soon there were many Western Sea men like that one here in Korea. They traveled to our land from Europe, as well as from America. But it was the people from America we liked the best. They were our friends, especially the 'Jesus-believers' who had only good will in their hearts. They told us of their God. They set up schools for our girls as well as for our boys. I went to one such 'wake-up' school for a whole year. I stopped because my old-fashioned grandmother did not approve. She quickly arranged with the go-between for my marriage to your grandfather.

"Best of all, the Americans brought us their magic medicine. It drove out the spirits of sickness far better than the charms of the most skillful *mudang*. Many a Korean life was saved by the American doctors in their 'sick-houses.'

"Thousands of men and women here followed the teaching of those 'Jesus-men.' The pocket I am sewing into this suit I am making for my brother, Yong Tu, is a 'Bible pocket.' It was invented by the followers of these 'Jesus-men' for carrying their precious *unmun* Bible. Yong Tu himself is not a 'Jesus-believer,' but a pocket like this is useful for other things besides a book.

"I can remember, too," Ok Cha would say, "the very first jinriksha the Japanese brought to our city of Seoul. We called it *illukku* in Korean. The chair porters liked to run between its small shafts. Its light seat, set between the two smoothly running wheels, was far easier to manage than a sedan chair slung between heavy poles. One man could easily pull a jinriksha, even when a fat *yangban* sat in it.

The chair porters even preferred this new kind of vehicle to the ancient monocycle of the oldtime high officials. As they said, two wheels are always better than one."

"And bicycles, Halmoni?" one of Ok Cha's grandsons asked. "What did you think when you first saw a bicycle?"

"We called it a 'go-by-itself-wheel' because it needed no one at all to pull it. But the bicycle was not entirely new in our part of the world, at least my grandmother said so. She knew an old story about just such a two-wheeled affair that was invented long, long ago across the mountains in China.

"The bicycle in that story had two parts upon it, a 'go-part' and a 'come-back part,' " the Korean grandmother explained. "A man who owned such a bicycle was busy one day repairing the come-back part, which he had taken off. Now his old mother was curious about this strange riding machine. She greatly wanted to try it. And when she saw it leaning up against the open gate, she mounted upon its seat and rode away down the street. On and on, over the countryside she went. She had a fine ride, but when the sun dropped down behind the western mountains, she wanted to return home. Of course she could not, for the come-back part had been taken off the riding machine. The old woman was never seen again in that town. And that's why the dangerous 'go-by-itself-wheel' was given up in old China."

The children laughed merrily at this absurd story. They laughed, too, when their grandmother told them what people thought of the new solid coins that replaced the old copper cash. "We called them 'blind money,' " Ok Cha explained. "Without holes in their centers, we did not think they could be good coins. Without an eye, how can they see, we asked each other.

"When those first houses on wheels, called streetcars, appeared, people here were afraid that the spirits would be angry," the old woman remembered. "They threw stones at the car windows, and they tore up the rails. I know of one man who was killed because he jumped across the track in front of an oncoming car. He did that foolish thing hoping to escape himself, but hoping also that the car would run over any bad spirit that might be at his heels.

"It was the streetcar," Ok Cha continued, "that made our Emperor give orders that the city gates should no longer be closed with the ringing of the Great Bell. Indeed, very soon the Great Bell itself no longer rang to warn people in off the streets. With the city gates thrown wide open, men could travel whenever they liked, by night as well as by day.

"*Hé*, people went crazy about these strange new things from the West." Ok Cha shook her head as if she, too, had always known no good would come of giving up the ways of the Honorable Ancestors. "Men began to buy clothes like those of the foreigners. Some who had traveled in Western lands wore their hair as short as that of a priest. The Emperor even gave orders that all topknots should be cut off.

"But that was too much. Most of our men were proud of the neat knots under their fine hats of black gauze. How else could it be known when a boy became a man if he had not a topknot? The men refused to obey this order, and the Emperor did not insist. Of course, now that Western ideas, like the spirits, are everywhere in our land, all the boys and the young men cut their hair short. Your great uncle, Yong Tu, is the only man I know today who wears a topknot as a *yangban* should."

"But short hair is easier, and new ways are better, Halmoni," one of her granddaughters said. "I shouldn't like to stay all my life shut up in this Inner Court. I like to go to school. I like to play with my friends. I like picnics on the hills in the springtime. When I am older, I want to go to the Girls' University, Ewha, in Seoul."

"*Yé*, blessed girl, the new ways are better. Our people all say so. Those fire imps you call matches are safer than carrying a burning stick from a neighbor's fire to light the wood under our rice pots. The telegraph, the telephone, and the radio can give longer messages than the ancient signal fires on the mountains. On the smooth streets of our city we no longer need to walk upon high wooden shoes to keep our feet out of the mud. It's true that electric street lamps are far brighter than the paper lanterns our servants used to carry before us to light our steps.

"But there were many things about the days of my childhood that were good, too. Best of all, we were free. Our land belonged to us alone. Most of these new ways you like so well came during the dark years when Japan ruled our land.

"If you try to make friends with a tiger, you will soon find yourself in his stomach, my grandmother used to say." Ok Cha shook her head solemnly. "So it was with the Japanese. We let them come to us as friends. They remained as our enemies. They fought wars about us with China and Russia. And each time they won. At last, when they could, they took over our land and made it their own.

"*Ai-go! Ai-go!*" this old Korean grandmother moaned whenever she thought of those years under the cruel Japanese. The proud white Korean flag, with its round symbol of red and blue, was pulled down; the red and white flag of Japan flew over all buildings, both new and old. Even the name of the land was changed from Korea back to its ancient title, now spelled Chosen. Cities and towns were given Japanese names instead of their former Korean ones. The proud Koreans themselves were made into slaves. Even a *paksa* or a poet was punished if he did not work like a peasant for the dwarf men from Japan.

"Inside our gate the family had to crowd themselves into the servants' houses in the Outer Court. Japanese generals took over our home, and we had to serve them. The Japanese ate our food, and the 'Spring Hunger' lasted throughout the year. They would have stolen all our treasures if we had not buried them secretly out in the garden and under the *kimchee* jars." Ok Cha did not like to remember this part of her story.

"Terrible things happened then, my children. No man was safe—nor woman either. Never will I forget the sound of the Great Bell ringing again to warn the men off the streets at the time of the Korean revolution of 1919. Schoolgirls took part in this peaceful plea for independence. They loved their land quite as much as the singing girl, Nonga, in the old story. Along with the men they raised their voices out in the streets. They, too, shouted, '*Mansei! Mansei!*'—our old Korean battle cry which the Japanese had forbidden. Then it was that my husband, your grandfather, was beaten so badly that he went to the Distant Shore. He lost his life working for freedom for his country.

"Ai-go!" The old woman wiped a tear from her eye. "That revolution against the rule of Japan was foolish, I know. It was like trying to split a rock by throwing a hen's egg against it. The Japanese were too strong. They were too cruel. It was indeed a bad day when we let them into our land."

"But the Japanese are gone now, Halmoni. The American soldiers drove them out of Seoul as soon as the World War II was won." Thus one of the boys tried to comfort his sad old grandmother.

The older children of this household knew a great deal about the Japanese who had ruled over their country. They had learned early never to speak Korean words in their hearing. Those who went to the city schools had been forced to study their lessons in Japanese. They had to bow before the likeness of the Japanese Emperor, whom they must call the "Son of Heaven."

And they had to learn by heart the benefits which had come to their land under the Japanese: factories, with humming machines; fine stores and handsome government buildings of stone; modern hotels and department stores; thousands of trees planted upon the bare Korean hillsides; steel bridges over the rivers; automobiles rolling over smooth roads; and airplanes rising from airfields into the blue sky! All these, the Japanese boasted, were the gifts they had brought to their Korean colony.

"But they brought us also hunger and fear, sadness and suffering," Ok Cha always added when these benefits were mentioned. "They took our rice fields from us. They burned our precious books. They tried to make us forget our own language. And they killed our brave men."

The old grandmother's face always brightened when her grandsons spoke of the American soldiers. *"Hué,* it is good to think of those tall men in their brown suits," she said. "They gave us new hope, like spring blossoms sprouting from a dead branch at the winter's end. Their coming was as welcome as water flowing once more, after a rain, in the dry bed of a stream.

"Yé, my young dragons, the Americans gave us back our country. And we are grateful. *Mansei! Mansei!* May Korea live free for ten thousand years!"